Read more about Katie and her friends in the first book, *Little Big Sister*

"Little Big Sister is a gentle, winning story. It is especially well suited to classroom use."
- *Blueink Review*

"Beautifully and honestly written story of the reality of living with a sibling who has special needs."
- *Amazon Review*

Little Big Sister – Winner of the 2017 Next Generation Indie Book Awards

Little Big Sister

on the Move

Written by

Amy B. McCoy

For Peyton,
Stay Kind!

Ay McCoy

Illustrations by
Christine Maichin

Library of Congress Cataloging-in-Publication Data
McCoy, Amy B.
Little Big Sister on the Move / by Amy B. McCoy
p. cm.

Summary: Follow nine-year-old Katie and her family as they move to a
new home in a different state. Katie's big brother, Mikey has autism, and
she feels it's her responsibility to help new neighbors, friends and
community members understand autism better
ISBN 978-1-7330362-0-7

[1. Siblings – Fiction. 2. Family – Fiction. 3. Disabilities – Fiction.
4. Autism – Fiction. 5. Interpersonal Relationships – Fiction.] 1. Title

Printed in the United States of America

Dedicated to my parents, Sue and George Bashian, for their encouragement, support, and love throughout my life and for instilling a love of reading and writing in me through their own example.

Chapter One
Lost and Found

"Katie!" I could hear Mom's voice calling me from downstairs. *Wow, that's a change*, I thought to myself. *Mom is calling for me instead of me calling for her.* I was in my new room, unpacking the boxes that held the stuff for my desk. We'd just moved from Connecticut to New York for Dad's job, and unpacking all the boxes was taking forever.

I guess I was taking too long to answer Mom because I heard her shout, "Katie!" again, even louder this time. Mom really sounded upset. I could hear her footsteps echoing through the house as she walked up the stairs.

"What?" I finally answered back.

"I can't find Mikey. Have you seen him?" She was breathing quickly, the way my breathing sounds when I'm nervous.

"No, I've been unpacking like you asked me to," I replied. I was trying to figure out the best spot on my desk to keep my notebook collection. I was holding a stack of five notebooks, all filled with my lists. Making lists in notebooks is one of my favorite things to do.

"Katie, I really need your help," Mom pleaded. "Mikey doesn't know his way around our new neighborhood yet, and he's gone." I could tell she was trying to keep her voice steady.

Most nine-year-old *younger* sisters like me don't have to help their parents find their *older* brothers. But Mikey is not like most older brothers. Mikey has autism, so for him that means he acts more like he is six years old instead of eleven, which is his real age. So I usually have to act like the big sister. That's why my parents call me his little big sister.

"OK, I'll check the basement and back yard," I offered.

"I've looked in the basement and the back yard already. I've checked the entire house and every hiding spot I can think of," Mom said. "I need you to help me look for him outside in the neighborhood."

Oh no. Was she thinking of knocking on neighbors' doors? This was *not* how I pictured meeting our new neighbors. I could just imagine Mom saying to the neighbors: *Hi, we just moved in, and we've lost our son. Have you seen him? By the way, he has autism, so he might act differently than you expect.*

At our old house in Connecticut, we lived on a quiet street where we didn't have to worry much about cars driving by. Here in New York, our street is much busier. There are cars driving by all the time. I know Mom was worried about Mikey crossing the street without looking both ways first and getting hurt.

Mom and I walked out of our front door together. We looked up and down the block both ways and didn't see him.

I saw something blue in the grass. "Mom, look!" I pointed to the blue thing, which turned out to be Mikey's crocs in front of our neighbor's house.

Mom ran over to the shoes and picked them up. She held them to her heart as if they were a piece of Mikey. Then we walked up the short walkway to the neighbor's door together. Just as Mom was about to push the doorbell, her phone buzzed. "Look, Katie," she showed me her phone screen. There was a text message that just said, "Hi Mommy," from an unknown number. I know we were both thinking the same thing. That Mikey was texting us from someone's phone.

3

We rang the doorbell, but thankfully no one answered. I was relieved that I wouldn't have to meet the neighbors during our embarrassing search for Mikey since they weren't home. Just then, I thought I heard Mikey's silly, loud laugh. At the same time, Mom's phone buzzed again. It was another text from the same unknown number. This time when she showed me her phone screen, it said, "Hi Mommy Happy Happy Tremendous Tuesday."

"Mom, do you hear him laughing?" I asked.

She nodded as her face softened and she almost smiled. She got another text that said, "Mommy come find me." We followed the laughing sounds to the neighbor's backyard, which was where we found Mikey. He was alone, leaning back on a patio chair with his feet up on the table. He had a huge grin on his face and someone's phone in his hands.

"Hi, Mommy! Hi, Mommy! Hi, Mommy!" he said three times as usual. He seemed so excited to see us.

"Mikey, this is not our yard, and that is not your phone," Mom said. "Time to go home." She tried to make her voice sound like she was mad at him, but I could tell she was relieved we found him.

"No, Mommy. No, Mommy. No, Mommy," Mikey replied. "I like this phone!"

I heard a car pull into the neighbor's driveway. My heart raced—I was so embarrassed to be in their back yard. This was going to be such an awkward way to meet them.

Mom took a few steps from the back yard to their driveway and waved hello as the car stopped.

A woman about Mom's age got out of the car. "Hi! You must be our new neighbors. I'm Julie." She shook Mom's hand and smiled at me.

"Hi, Julie, it's so nice to meet you. I'm Anna, and this is my daughter, Katie." Mom said. "My son, Mikey is sitting in your back yard. I hope you don't mind."

"I don't mind at all! He can sit there for as long as he wants." Julie smiled as she looked over at Mikey. Julie had kind eyes and didn't look mad or surprised that we were in her driveway and back yard. "What grade are you going into, Katie?"

"Fourth," I told her. She was so nice. She didn't even ask why Mikey was sitting in her backyard. She acted like she always pulled her car into her driveway and found perfect strangers there.

"My daughter, Caroline, will be in fourth grade too. She's going to be so happy when she finds out you moved in next door. She's always hoped for a girl neighbor her age since all she has at home are older brothers."

That sounded a lot like me last year. I had always wished for a neighbor my age when we lived in Connecticut, and then Lauren moved in just two houses away. Could I really get so lucky again?

"Mikey, come say hello to our new neighbor, Mrs.—what is your last name?" Mom turned to Julie.

"The kids can just call me Julie," she said.

"Hi, Julie! I have your phone, phone, phone!" Mikey said.

Julie smiled and asked, "How old are you, Mikey?"

"Ten," he said.

Why does he always forget how old he is? I wondered to myself, rolling my eyes.

"You're not ten anymore, Mikey. Remember, you already had your birthday," Mom reminded him.

"Eleven," he tried again. He held up the phone and smiled at Julie.

"Mikey, thanks for finding my phone!" Julie said. "I was just at my son's soccer game. When I got there, I realized I'd forgotten my phone, so I rushed back home to get it. I'm so glad I did because I got to meet you all. Where did you find my phone, Mikey?"

"Patio, patio, patio," he replied.

Then, something unusual happened. Mikey stood up, walked over to Julie, and handed her the phone. I've never seen Mikey give someone their phone back so quickly and without being told to do it a hundred times. Usually, he holds on to phones and electronics for as long as he can.

"Low battery, low battery, low battery," he told us as he hopped on the grass between our house and Julie's. The houses and yards are so much closer together here in New York than what I was used to in Connecticut. In about three short hops, he was in our yard.

Julie took a look at her screen. "Anna, it looks like Mikey added your name and number into my contacts as 'Mommy's cell phone'! Wow, he is really good with phones, huh?"

People always think Mikey is good with phones since he is quick to add contacts. She had no idea how many phones he has messed up over the years. I was just glad he didn't break hers.

Julie was getting back into her car to go out again. "And Mikey was right about the low battery. It's only on ten percent," she told us as she held up her phone.

Now I know why he gave the phone back so easily. He doesn't like when the battery is so low.

"Have a great day. So nice to meet you, Julie," Mom said. She smiled at me, and the worried look was completely gone from her eyes. I was glad I'd been able to help her find Mikey.

"Bye, Anna," Julie said to Mom. Then she looked at Mikey and said, "Thanks again for finding my phone, Mikey."

"Bye! Bye! Bye!" Mikey said with a hop for each word.

Then Julie looked at me and said, "Katie, I'll come by with Caroline to meet you later today when she gets home from her play practice."

"OK, thanks," I said.

As she pulled out of her driveway, she waved at us from her open car window. Mikey yelled, "Beep, beep, beep!" He always yells that when cars drive by, and he gets so excited when people actually beep their horns for him. Julie heard him, and she beeped as she drove away. Mikey did what Dad calls his triple hop of happiness. Then he started to flap his arms which is the other thing he does when he feels happy and excited. Mom calls it smiling with his whole body when he jumps and flaps like that. And I was surprised that I didn't even feel embarrassed. Julie seemed to "get it" about Mikey already.

Hopes and Wishes

I hope I make new friends easily and quickly in NY

I wish we didn't have to move

I hope Mikey learns how to act his age one day

I wish Mikey didn't have autism

Chapter Two
Pizza and Settling In

That afternoon, Mom took Mikey and me out for lunch. There were some workers at the house painting the family room and dining room, so Mom wanted to get out of the house while they were working. I think she also wanted to make sure Mikey wouldn't touch the walls while they were still wet with paint. Or worse, try to "help" the painters, which would not be any help at all.

We found a great pizza place that Mom had read about in the local newspaper. The restaurant had gluten-free pizza for Mikey and the best breadsticks I've ever tasted. By the time we got there, it was after lunch time but before dinner time, so the restaurant wasn't crowded at all. Mom has told me that she likes to take Mikey to restaurants only when they're not busy since crowded places are too loud for him. I also like going to restaurants when they're less busy, since there are fewer pairs of eyes to stare at us.

Once we sat down, Mikey asked his embarrassing questions to our server.

"What's your name, name, name?" he asked.

"I'm Erin, what's your name?" She smiled at him. She looked like she was in high school.

He didn't answer her. He just went on with his own list of questions. "What time do you go to work?"

Mom interrupted, "Mikey, Erin asked you a question. First answer her. Tell her your name."

"I'm Mikey, Mikey, Mikey. What time do you go to work?"

"I work here from noon until five today," Erin said.

I know Mom is always talking to him about appropriate and inappropriate questions. Asking someone you don't even know what time they work is definitely inappropriate. I wish he wouldn't ask that one.

Mikey continued with his inappropriate questions. "Do you work here every day?"

"No, not every day, just on Tuesdays and Wednesdays in the summer," Erin answered patiently. She was still smiling at him—it was a real smile, not one of those fake ones. She was holding a pad of paper and a pen, ready to take our order, but Mikey kept interrupting her.

"OK, Mikey, that's enough questions. Let's order our food," Mom announced. I was glad she stopped him. I think he would go on all day asking questions if Mom hadn't ended it. Erin didn't seem to mind, though.

"Katie, you go first, first, first!" Mikey said.

Mom smiled and said to Erin, "I hope you don't mind, but Mikey likes to be in charge of who orders their food first, and he always likes to go last."

"That's fine with me," Erin said as she turned to me to take my lunch order. I noticed she was wearing a blue puzzle piece necklace. Now I knew why she got it. Puzzle pieces are a sign of autism awareness.

* * * * * *

We liked the pizza so much we brought some home for dinner. Pizza is my favorite food, so it was fine with me to have it for both lunch and dinner.

When we got home, the painters were finished, but I noticed our house smelled like new paint. "Mom, when will that paint smell go away?" I asked. *Ugh, it smelled gross!*

"If we keep the windows open to air out the house,

it will go away in a day or so," she said.

I was hoping our new house wouldn't always have the smell of new paint. Lauren's house smelled like tomato sauce because her mom is an awesome cook and makes sauce with tomatoes from her own garden. My grandparents' house smelled like coffee because they make coffee a lot. Every house has its own smell, but I've always wondered why you can't smell what your own house smells like. Maybe it's because you get used to it.

Every house has its own sounds too. I know our house is loud because of the noises Mikey makes, but I barely hear him anymore because I'm used to the sounds he makes. When I was younger and had friends over, some of them would tell me that my house was loud. That always hurt my feelings. As my friends got to know Mikey, most of them started to understand that his noises were a part of his autism. Just thinking of starting over again with new friends in a new town made my breathing get fast and my stomach feel funny.

I went to my room to take some deep breaths and tried to finish unpacking. In my hand, I held a framed picture that my best friends, Lauren and Bella, gave me as a going-away gift. In the picture, the three of us are standing together at my old school on the day we gave our first presentation about disabilities. I wanted to find the perfect spot to hang the picture in my new room. Mom tried to make it feel comfortable and familiar by getting the walls painted the same turquoise color as my room in Connecticut. But it was still hard to get used to everything being new. As I looked at the gift from Lauren and Bella, the picture made me realize how much I missed them already.

I know it might sound strange to think about going back to school in the middle of summer, but I was looking forward to starting fourth grade at my new school. This would be my first time being in a school *without* Mikey. At my old school, everyone knew me as "Mikey's sister." He's one of those kids that everyone knows because he's so friendly and talks to everyone. Kids at my old school also knew him because he had a few meltdowns in the hallways. But here in Fairview City, our new town, Mikey is going to the middle school, and I'll be at the elementary school. No one at my new school will have to know what a loud and embarrassing brother I have! I will get to be "Katie" instead of "Mikey's sister."

I remember last year, before my friends and I did our presentation about disabilities at school, how uncomfortable I used to feel during lunch. While Mikey was at recess outside with the other fourth graders, I was eating lunch in the cafeteria with the third graders. He would mush his face up against the window from outside and say, "Hi, Katie! Hi, Katie! Hi, Katie!" Through the window, his face always looked lost or confused because he had his mouth half way open. I would want to disappear. My friends would say, "Look, Katie, there's Mikey!" as if I'd be excited to see him. Nope. Not excited at all. They'd smile and wave at him till he smiled back. But I could hear the boys at the lunch table next to mine laugh at him and try to copy the look on his face. It made me so mad. But at my new school, I won't have to worry about being embarrassed.

Some embarrassing things about Mikey

He asks so many questions to strangers (especially to servers at restaurants)

He has a confused look on his face -with his mouth half open a lot of the time

He asks people who drive by our house to beep their car horns

Chapter Three
Hello Neighbors

I heard the front door open as Dad yelled, "Is anyone home?" Dad always asks that when he gets home from work, even when he knows we're home. It's his way of saying, "I'm home!" and I love that he still did it in our new house.

I ran down to greet him. "How was work at your new office, Dad?"

"Good. I like my new office. Thanks for asking, Katie," Dad replied. "How was your day in the new house?"

"Well," I started listing what we did that day. "I finished unpacking my room, we met our next-door neighbor, we found a good pizza place for lunch, and Mikey only got lost once." I put that last detail in to see if he was listening.

"I can't wait to see how you arranged your room. I'm glad you found a good pizza place. And how did Mikey get lost? What happened?" Dad *is* a good listener.

"Mom couldn't find him anywhere, but together we found him in the neighbor's back yard."

"Oh," said Dad as he walked up the stairs. "So he was right next door all along?"

"Yup."

"Do you want to help me find our bikes and sports equipment in the garage after we eat dinner?" Dad asked. "Then maybe we can take a bike ride later and explore the neighborhood."

I really didn't feel like helping in the garage. It was a huge mess full of boxes waiting to be unpacked. But I did want to ride my bike, so I told Dad I would help out.

"Daddy! Daddy! Daddy!" Mikey came barreling out of his room to say hello to Dad. I wonder when he is going to stop calling him *Daddy* and start calling him *Dad* like most kids his age.

"Hey, buddy, how was your day?" Dad asked as Mikey gave him a giant hug in the upstairs hallway outside his room.

"Pizza, pizza, pizza," Mikey replied. Sometimes he doesn't answer questions directly and just says what he wants to say.

"Thanks for reminding me, Mikey," Mom called from the kitchen. "There's pizza for dinner from the new pizza place we discovered today. They even had gluten-free pizza for Mikey and me."

"Sounds delish," Dad said.

After our quick pizza dinner, Dad and I headed out to the garage. We were looking through boxes for our bike helmets. We had already found our bikes and the basketball. I started bouncing the ball when I saw Julie with her daughter walking up our driveway. I waved and felt my heartbeat speed up, but I wasn't as nervous as I was this morning when we were in Julie's driveway.

"Hi, Katie, this is Caroline," Julie said.

"Hi," I said with a smile. I wanted to seem really friendly even though I'm usually shy at first. I thought of last year, meeting Lauren for the first time when she moved in to her house on our street, and how friendly she was. I clearly remembered how she made me feel when we first met. She was so smiley and kind, and she made me feel like I wanted to become friends with her immediately. I hoped I was making Caroline feel that way about me.

"Hi," Caroline said back. She didn't look up at me. She looked at the ground. She seemed shy too. I could definitely relate to that.

"You must be Julie," said Dad, walking out of the garage and then shaking her hand. "Anna and Katie told me all about the phone incident today. I'm sorry about that. I'm Grant." Dad and Julie began to talk.

"So, are you going into fourth grade?" Caroline asked me.

"Yes," I replied, "what about you?" Even though her mom already told me that we're both going into fourth grade, I couldn't think of anything else to ask.

"Me too," she said. "Maybe we'll be in the same class."

I smiled and nodded.

Just then, I heard the back door slam as Mikey ran out shouting, "Julie, Julie, Julie!" He darted right over to her so he could give her a hug. It was the kind of hug people give to friends or relatives that they've known their whole lives. And when Mikey hugs, it's usually the kind that almost knocks you down. Caroline looked a little surprised to see Mikey hug her mom so tight. But Julie hugged him right back as if they'd been friends forever.

"What's your phone on?" Mikey asked Julie when he finally released her from the hug. He always holds hugs for a few seconds too long.

"What?" Julie asked.

I could tell she wanted to make sure she understood him. Sometimes it's hard to understand the way Mikey talks. He has something called apraxia, which is a speech disorder. He didn't learn to talk till he was five. He's been going to speech therapy since he was a baby. First it was to learn to talk, and now he goes to help him with things like staying on topic in conversations. I hardly notice that he sounds different when he talks since I'm so used to the way he sounds.

"What's your phone on?" Mikey repeated.

"It's on my counter." Julie smiled. "In my kitchen."

"No. No. No. What is your phone on? What number? What number? What number?" Mikey tried hard to make Julie understand what he wanted to know. I knew what he was asking.

Dad said, "I think he wants to know what percent battery your phone is on."

"Yes! Yes! Yes!" Mikey started jumping. I think he was excited that he was going to get an answer.

Why was he so embarrassing? I know that no one else really asks people what percent their battery is on since it's such an unusual question. It's such a Mikey question. I glanced over at Caroline and noticed that she looked at Mikey with the same kind smile that her Mom had. I took a deep breath of relief.

Then Julie answered his question like it was something she was asked every day. "My phone's on

86 percent. Much better than this morning, right, Mikey?"

Mikey started doing his triple hop of happiness and flapping his hands. He was smiling with his whole body. *I don't think I will ever understand why knowing battery percents is so exciting to him.*

"Who is this?" Mikey moved closer to Caroline and touched her shoulder.

Dad moved so he stood in between Caroline and Mikey and gently moved Mikey's hand off Caroline's shoulder. He reminded him, "Personal space, buddy."

"Mikey, this is my daughter, Caroline," said Julie.

"Hi, Mikey," Caroline said. This time she looked up and smiled.

"Caroline, Caroline, Caroline," Mikey said. "Now I know *two* Carolines!" He always tells us how many people he knows with the same name. He has a good friend in Connecticut named Caroline.

"Caroline, why don't you take Katie to our back yard. You girls can jump on the trampoline," Julie said. *Thank you, Julie,* I thought to myself. I was so happy for this escape from more embarrassing moments with Mikey.

"OK, Mom," said Caroline. "Do you want to jump on my trampoline?" she asked me.

I smiled. "Can I go, Dad?"

"Sure. We'll go on a bike ride another time," he said.

Caroline and I ran over to her yard. Once we were bouncing on her trampoline, it was so much easier to talk.

"How old is Mikey?" she asked.

"He's eleven," I replied.

"He seems really friendly. My mom said he likes phones and when cars beep their horns."

"Your mom's right," I said. "Mikey does love those things.

"My mom used to be a teacher, so she knows a lot about kids," Caroline said in between trampoline jumps. "Now she stays at home to take care of my brothers and me."

So that explained why Julie was so good with Mikey—she used to be a teacher, just like Mom. "How old are your brothers?" I asked as I bounced really high on the trampoline.

"Tommy is eleven, and Nick is fourteen. But they're never home. Especially in the summer. They're always at soccer. Or lacrosse. Or golf practice. Or my dad takes them to baseball games. My mom jokes that they only come home to eat and sleep." Caroline laughed. "The rest of the time they're playing sports or watching sports. Sometimes I feel like an only child."

"I have the exact opposite problem. Mikey is *always* home. He doesn't go anywhere unless we all go," I told Caroline. "Since he has special needs, he doesn't really play sports like your brothers."

"One of my brothers is on a Unified Basketball team. He always says that of all the teams he's on, Unified Basketball is his favorite. He's a partner to a boy on the team who has special needs. Maybe Mikey can join that team?" She looked at me for a moment and then said, "You know, since you mentioned Mikey has special needs."

"He'd probably like that. We had Unified Sports in our old town in Connecticut. We both played on our school's team."

"What kind of special needs does he have?" she asked.

My legs stopped bouncing. I was thinking of what I should say next.

"I'm so sorry, I shouldn't have asked. That was so rude of me." I noticed her face had turned bright red, and she looked down.

"No, it wasn't rude at all. It's totally fine to ask me about Mikey," I told her. "He has autism." I paused again. "I'm glad you asked. I like teaching people about it."

Caroline

She's easy to talk to

I'm glad she's my neighbor

She's friendly and kind

Even though I just met her,
I have a feeling that we
will become good friends

Chapter Four
Special Drink

"Katie! Mikey!" Mom called. "It's time for breakfast."

I heard Mikey stomp down the stairs. He loves breakfast and always eats the same thing every day. Three scrambled eggs with gluten-free toast. I took my time getting downstairs. I've learned that if I time it just right, Mikey will be finished eating his eggs and toast as I sit down to eat my cereal and fruit. And that's what I wanted. For him to leave the kitchen so I could eat my breakfast in peace and quiet.

As I was entering the kitchen, I knew I timed it just right because I heard Mom say, "Good job eating all your eggs, Mikey. Now it's time for your special drink."

"Special drink. Special drink. Special drink," Mikey said as he hopped to the counter. Mom had just placed a mini red cup down for him. This was his special drink.

"Stand still, and it won't spill." Mom always sings this little rhyme to him just as she hands him the mini cup and watches him drink it. "Good job, Mikey!"

"All done, iPad time!" Mikey said. Off he ran to grab his iPad from the counter, and I heard him screech with delight from the living room. He must have had an email from one of his favorite teachers in Connecticut, Mrs. Strickland or Mrs. Oh.

I sat down and poured the milk into my cereal bowl. "I was wondering, Mom, why does Mikey have to drink that special drink every day?" Before she could answer, I asked my next question: "And do you have a special drink for me?" For as long as I could remember, Mikey has his special drink after breakfast and after dinner every day.

"Mikey's special drink is medicine," Mom said.

"Oh, is he sick?" I asked, my mouth full of cereal.

"No, he's not sick. This medicine is not what you'd take for a sore throat or a fever. It's a different type of medicine," she said.

"What kind of medicine is it then?" I asked.

"Mikey has epilepsy. That means he has seizures. The medicine stops the seizures from happening," Mom explained.

"What are seizures again?" I asked. I knew I'd heard Mom and Dad talk about seizures before, but I wasn't quite sure what they were.

Mom took a sip of her coffee and explained, "A seizure is when the brain is not able to control what the body does for a few minutes. So if Mikey had a seizure, his eyes would close, he would probably be on the ground, and his body would shake all over," Mom said. "He wouldn't be aware that it was happening."

"Does Mikey get hurt when he has a seizure?" I asked.

"Mikey's never hurt himself when he's had seizures." Mom continued. "We've been lucky. So far, Mikey's seizures have happened in his car seat, sitting on the couch and in other safe and soft places."

I put my spoon down and wiped my mouth with a napkin. "Mom, will I ever get epilepsy? You know, since Mikey has it, does it run in our family?" I held my breath as I waited for Mom's answer, hoping she would say no.

"Epilepsy doesn't run in our family. Mikey's the only one who has it in our family. You will not get epilepsy just because Mikey has it."

Phew! I felt myself exhale with relief. "When was the last time Mikey had a seizure?"

"It was about six years ago."

"What was it like?" I asked.

"You were there, Katie, so maybe you remember a little bit, but you were only three at the time. We were in the car, and he started shaking in his car seat. I was backing out of the driveway, and you said in your cute, three-year-old voice, 'Mommy, look at Mikey. What is Mikey doing?' I turned around and saw Mikey shaking with his eyes closed. I realized he was having a seizure, so I drove right back into the driveway and turned off the car. I quickly got out of the driver's seat, then opened the back door so I could get close to Mikey. I wanted to make sure he didn't have anything in his mouth."

"Why were you doing that?" I asked.

"Good question, Katie. So he didn't choke," Mom explained. "In the moment when you watch someone you love having a seizure, it can look scary since their body isn't in control," she explained. "The seizure lasted about two minutes, and then he fell asleep. That's what happens after a seizure. The person having it feels very tired and usually doesn't remember that the seizure even happened."

"When will he have his next seizure?" I asked.

"We never know when a seizure is going to happen. That's another hard thing about seizures. We can't plan for them," Mom said.

"Well, since he takes medication, why does he still have seizures at all?" I asked.

"That's a mystery, but he has an appointment with his neurologist, Dr. Levy, every three months. She makes sure he's taking the right amount of medicine as his body grows," Mom explained.

I was still a little bit confused but glad I'd asked about seizures.

Mom changed the subject. "I haven't had a chance to ask you yet—how was your time with Caroline on her trampoline yesterday?"

"Good. I just hope we get the same teacher so I have a friend in my class."

"I hope so too. You're good at making new friends, Katie," Mom said.

"Caroline said we can walk to school together when school starts," I told her. "And she's going to be in a play next week. Can we go watch her?"

"Of course, that sounds like fun. Maybe we can all go together as a family."

I looked at her, wondering why she always thinks Mikey will be able to do things that are impossible for him. Things like sitting still watching a play or even going to the movies. I was about to tell her no way, I wasn't going to watch Caroline's play with Mikey. Then she looked at me as if reading my mind and said,

"Or maybe just you and I can go to the play together and make it a girls' night out. I doubt Mikey will be able to sit through it anyway."

Mikey was still in the living room on his iPad sending emails to his friends and teachers in Connecticut. I could hear that he was also on our house phone talking to Nana. Mom lets him use the house phone to call Nana every morning. Talking on the phone is definitely one of his favorite things to do, especially when the phone call is with Nana. I'm so glad he was on the phone since it gave a moment of quiet for Mom and me to talk without him interrupting.

Wondering

I wonder if Mikey will ever
have another seizure
(I hope not)

I wonder what it feels like
to have a seizure

I wonder how many other
kids with autism have
seizures

Chapter Five
The Grocery Store

"Katie, will you help me make a list of snacks that you'd like to have in the pantry?" Mom handed me a pen and a pad of paper.

"OK," I said as I sat down at the kitchen counter. I know she wanted me to include healthy snacks like pretzels, apples, and almonds. But I made sure to also write some of my favorites like Oreos, ice cream, and brownie mix.

"Let's get the shopping done this morning so we'll have time to go to the pool this afternoon," Mom said as she sat down next to me to make her own list for the grocery store. Then, she said loud enough for Mikey to hear from where he was sitting at the kitchen table, "Mikey, in five minutes it's time to put your iPad away and get ready to go to the store."

No reply from Mikey. He was in his own world. That happens a lot.

Mom walked over to him and put her face right next to his and gently touched his shoulder. "Mikey, look at me." He looked up. "We're going to the store together in five minutes. Please make a list of snacks you want to buy."

I stopped writing my list and asked, "Mom are you kidding me? Do we have to bring Mikey with us? He is so embarrassing to be with in stores."

"Katie, we're new here." Mom looked up at me when she added, "I don't know any sitters yet, so of course Mikey's coming with us." She sounded a little bit frustrated.

Mikey usually does lots of embarrassing things when we go shopping together with Mom. I remember one time he had a meltdown at the mall when we left the computer store before he wanted to leave. Mom had to sing to calm him down and get him out of the store and into the car.

Another time we were in CVS together buying some vitamins and Mikey's special drink (which I now realize is his seizure medication). Mom had finished paying and tried to get him to walk out of the store, when all of a sudden, the song "Sweet Home Alabama" started playing in the store. Mikey loves

"Sweet Home Alabama," so we were stuck in the store till the song ended. The embarrassing part is that Mikey started singing along. LOUDLY. Everyone who walked by us stared at him. But once a song starts that Mikey likes, he can't do anything until the song is over. If we're in the car and get to our destination but a song he likes is playing, he won't get out of the car till the song ends. Mom says it's one of his "autism things." I say it's one of his "annoying things."

There was also the time he refused to go into the post office when Mom had to mail an important package. He lay on the ground outside of the post office in the parking lot, saying, "No pos-offit, no pos-offit, no pos-offit." That's how he said "post office" back then. Mom asked me to hold the small package she was planning to mail while she tried to peel Mikey off the ground. Luckily, a good friend of Mom's walked by at that moment and mailed the package for her so we didn't have to go into the post office after all.

Even though Mikey is hard to be with in public, he actually likes going to the grocery store. He always finds something new at the grocery store that he wants to try. He calls it "my pick." When Mom tells him that we're going to the store, he immediately asks, "Can I get my pick?" Mom lets him choose something if he listens and follows her store rules.

Mom and I had finished making our lists and were ready to walk out the door. She asked Mikey to show her his list. Mikey doesn't write by holding a pen or pencil. He has trouble holding the pencil. He either holds it too tight or too loose. He can write his name with a pencil, but by the time he gets to the L in MICHAEL, his hand is tired. And it sort of looks like a three-year-old wrote the letters. He goes to OT, which means occupational therapy, to help with his handwriting and other skills that are hard for him. Many kids who have autism go to OT to get help. So instead of writing with a pencil on paper, he writes by typing on his iPad. He can type words faster than anyone I know.

Mom turned to Mikey and said, "That's a great list. I know you're going to be safe and helpful while we're shopping in the store." She paused and told him, "Mikey, let's read your store rules."

Mikey's Store Rules

1. Stay close to Mom (do not wander)
2. Use your walking feet (no running away)
3. Help Mom find items on the list

Mom always does this with Mikey before we leave the house. When I asked her once why she does this, she said most kids with autism need to be reminded of how to stay safe and what to expect before they go out. She called it "previewing." She goes over rules with him before we leave for other places, too, like the pool, church, restaurants, or even birthday parties. Sometimes it works. Other times, it doesn't work at all. I really hoped it would work today.

We arrived at the grocery store and started loading up our cart. Mikey remembered most of the time to stay next to Mom and only had to be reminded once or twice to stop running.

Mom and I were checking over our lists while

Mikey wandered up the chips aisle. He started jumping up and down, saying, "Daddy's chips, Daddy's chips, Daddy's chips!" in his very loud and excited voice. He had spotted the yellow bag of potato chips that Dad always eats with his sandwich for lunch on weekends. He got right up close to the chips and just stared at the yellow bags all lined up on the shelf. Not moving, not jumping anymore. Just staring. He was in his own world.

An older woman came up next to him and said, "Excuse me, young man." It was obvious to me that she was trying to reach the chips that Mikey was staring at, but he was standing in the way. "Excuse me," she said a little louder this time. Mikey didn't even know she was there next to him. He was in his own world where only Daddy's favorite potato chips existed.

"Hey, don't ignore me while I'm talking to you." The woman sounded annoyed. "I've asked you to move out of my way two times."

I wanted to run over there and tell the lady to leave Mikey alone. I wanted to tell her that he couldn't help it. I wanted to tell her that autism makes kids like Mikey look like they understand how to communicate. But really, Mikey and others with autism can easily go into their own world where they have no idea of what is going on around them.

I saw the lady start to walk away as she said something else to Mikey that I couldn't hear. Mom saw the whole thing. She said, "Katie, stay here and keep an eye on Mikey for a minute." Mom walked over to where the woman had moved to and said, "Were you talking to my son just now?"

"Yes, he ignored me," the woman said. "I asked him to move over so I could reach the chips, and he didn't move. He acted like I wasn't even there."

"Do you have a minute for me to tell you about him?" Mom said calmly.

The lady nodded.

"He has autism," Mom said.

The lady stopped looking annoyed and started looking interested in what Mom was saying.

"So when you say he acted like you weren't there, you're right. He does go into his own world and can be unaware of what's happening around him." Mom sounded like a nice teacher helping a student understand a difficult subject.

"Well, it sounds like I owe your son an apology," the lady said. "And I want to thank you for explaining about how people with autism go into their own worlds."

"You're welcome," Mom said.

"I guess I have a lot to learn about autism." The mean lady was not so mean anymore. She had softened up.

"Thank you for listening to me," Mom said.

And that was that. Mom made a difference. She taught the lady about autism.

* * * * * *

When we got home from the grocery store, I tried to help Mom put away the food, but I really didn't know which drawers and cabinets everything went in yet. "Mom, why did you say something about Mikey to that lady in the store?"

"One of my jobs as Mikey's mom is to help people understand autism better. People who don't live with autism really can't be expected to understand. Mikey is going to grow up and become an adult with autism." Mom looked at me and said, "I think helping others understand about autism will make the world a better place for Mikey and other people like him."

"I can't really imagine Mikey as an adult, Mom. Do you think he will ever get married?"

She was concentrating on putting the groceries away and didn't respond right away. Finally, she said, "I've seen that there are many people with special needs who get married."

"Really? Who would marry him? Would it be someone who also has autism?"

"Well, Mikey would have to be in love with the person, and the person would have to be in love with him. That's how getting married works," Mom replied.

"Eww! That's gross, Mom," I said.

She laughed. "*If* Mikey does fall in love when he's an adult and *if* he wants to get married, we would figure out a way to make that happen for him," Mom said.

Wow. I was sort of shocked. I really can't imagine Mikey as an adult. It kind of feels like he will always be a child. "Mom, do you think Mikey will ever get his driver's license?" Sometimes I hear him say things like, *Mommy, when I grow up, I am going to drive a blue car.*

Mom said, "There are a lot of rules about driving that Mikey doesn't understand. And there are difficult tests that new drivers have to study for and pass before getting a driver's license."

"So does that mean no?" I asked.

"I don't like to limit what Mikey can or can't do in his future. Right now he lacks the safety skills needed to become a driver."

"That means, no, right?" I asked again.

"Katie…I can't imagine Mikey driving a car when he's an adult. But right now he's only eleven. He has several years to grow and mature before he becomes driving age," Mom said.

I was on a roll with my questions, and I had one more on my mind. I decided to go for it. "Mom, do you think Mikey will be able to go to college?"

"I know there are colleges that have special needs programs for students like Mikey," she said.

"But do you think he would be able to really do that?" I asked. "Can he really go to college?"

"I don't know yet," Mom said. "We'll find an opportunity that's right for him when he gets to the age of a college student."

Questions

Will Mikey ever get married?

Will Mikey ever drive a car?

Will Mikey go to college?

What job will Mikey have when he gets older?

Chapter Six
Mikey, The Neighborhood Watch

After we finished putting the groceries away, Mom made sandwiches for lunch. She asked me to set the patio table in the back yard with paper plates and napkins so we could sit outside and eat lunch.

We tried to eat our sandwiches out on the patio, but Mikey would not sit still in the back yard. He kept running to the front yard. He was only interested in one thing: watching the neighbors pull their cars into and out of their driveways. I don't know why, but that is one of his favorite things to do. Mikey was able to see lots of driveways from the front yard of our new house. He was taking his "job" as the Neighborhood Watch, which he started when we lived in Connecticut, to a whole new level.

"Katie, I have to follow Mikey to the front yard," Mom said as she ran around the side of the house, holding the rest of her sandwich wrapped in a napkin. "He can't be there alone. I don't know if he'll be safe."

Once again, Mom had to leave me to go check on Mikey. I found myself sitting alone in the back yard, eating my sandwich. I was used to Mom having to always check on Mikey, but I still felt annoyed.

"Bring your lunch and come keep me company," Mom yelled to me from the front of the house.

I followed Mom to the front yard. So much for setting the table on the patio. We were sitting side by side on the cement stoop in front of our house with paper plates in our laps. "Mom, do we really have to sit here?"

"Katie, I wish we could sit in the back yard too. But Mikey has to watch the cars. You know how much he enjoys being the Neighborhood Watch," she told me. "And I have to make sure he doesn't run into the street."

He is so annoying. He was sitting on the edge of our grass yelling, "Beep, beep, beep!" to all the cars driving by as he waved at them. Some of them did beep their horns, and he cheered for them.

"I don't get it," I said. "How can he sit and watch this for hours like it's an amazing show, but he can't sit through a movie?"

"I don't get it either, Katie. But most kids with autism have certain interests that others wouldn't find exciting at all," Mom explained. "I think his brain tells him that watching cars is the most important thing to do."

That reminded me of Adam from my old class. He memorized the entire flight schedule for Southwest Airlines. He could tell us what times the flights left the airport to fly to any city we named for him. That was his interest, memorizing flight times.

Mom finished her sandwich, and was switching her attention between making sure Mikey wasn't running into the street and glancing through Fairview City's local newspaper. Every now and then, she would point something out to me from the newspaper. "Look, here's a picture of the pool. We should join today."

"Mmm-hmmm," I replied. The picture she showed me looked awesome. A huge pool with water slides. *Going to the pool does sound like fun…if I had any friends to go with*, I thought to myself but didn't say to her.

Something or someone caught Mikey's attention because he started his triple hop of happiness. It was a lady walking her dog. They were approaching our house. I felt that feeling in my stomach as I watched

Mikey run over to her. "What's your name? Name? Name?"

"Hi. I'm Sally, and this is my dog, Lucky. What's your name?"

"Mikey! Mikey! Mikey!" he said. He started to reach toward Lucky, but Mom made it there just in time to take his hand.

"Mikey, be gentle with the dog," Mom said.

Gentle? I don't think he knows the meaning of that word.

Before Mom could introduce herself, Mikey was on to his next question. "Where are you going? Going? Going?" Mikey asked Sally.

"I'm taking Lucky for a walk, and then I'm going home," Sally answered. "You just moved in, right? I saw the moving truck here last week."

"Hi, I'm Anna." Mom extended her arm so they could shake hands. "Yes, you're right. We just moved in."

"Welcome to the neighborhood! We live down the block, so you'll see me outside walking with Lucky a lot!" Sally sounded friendly.

I walked over to stand next to Mom. "Mikey, is this your sister?" Sally asked.

But Mikey was jumping and flapping and all excited about a car pulling out of a driveway. He didn't even hear Sally's question. He was in his own world.

"This is my daughter, Katie," Mom said. I smiled at Sally.

"Hi, Katie. Let me guess, are you nine?"

"Yes," I said.

"Great! So is my daughter, Ella. She'll be so happy to meet you! Next time I'm walking Lucky, I'll bring her with me."

"Beep! Beep! Beep!" Mikey was yelling at the neighbors who had just pulled out of their driveway. The neighbors must have heard him because they beeped. Mikey jumped up and down, and his legs reminded me of a pogo stick. Sally laughed, but not like she was laughing at Mikey. She was laughing because it really was funny to see Mikey get so excited about a car horn beeping.

I stood there and petted Lucky behind his ears while Mom and Sally talked.

"Have you joined the Fairview City Pool yet?" Sally asked Mom.

"Not yet. I was just reading about it in the local paper," Mom replied.

"It's a great place for kids and families," Sally said. "I think you'll all like it there."

"We're planning to go there this afternoon to join," Mom said.

"Great, I'll see you there sometime soon, maybe even this afternoon," Sally said. Lucky started walking and pulled Sally to let her know he wanted to move again. "I have to finish Lucky's walk, but I'll see you guys soon. Bye! So nice to meet you!"

"Bye," Mom and I said at the same time. Mom added, "Nice to meet you too!"

Mikey didn't say good-bye. He was looking down the street in the other direction. Mom said, "Time to say good-bye, Mikey."

He was in his own world, so focused on anticipating the next car driving by or the next person walking by our house. He barely muttered, "Bye, bye, bye."

Mom and I were back on the stoop, and Mikey sat on the grass closer to the street. He wanted a front-row seat for the action in the neighborhood. A moment later, something new had caught his attention. It was the mail truck. He stood up and started jumping up and down saying, "Mail time, mail time, mail time!" The mail truck had parked a few houses down from ours, and the mailman was getting out of the truck. He had a large bag and started walking from house to house to deliver the mail. At our old house, Sheryl, the mail woman didn't get out of her truck. She put the mail in the mailboxes at the end of each driveway while staying in her truck. Here, the mailman had to walk from door to door to put letters through a mail slot because there were no mailboxes at the end of the driveways. This was new for Mikey (and for me).

Mikey was fascinated as he watched the mailman walk from house to house delivering the mail. His eyes were glued to the mailman as he said, "Mommy, Mommy, Mommy! Look! Look! Look!"

"Yes, Mikey. This mailman is walking to deliver the mail instead of driving like Sheryl did," Mom told him. "It's another new thing for us to get used to."

Mikey smiled his huge smile. I think that was his way of thanking Mom for explaining what he wanted to say but couldn't put into his own words.

"Coming to my house, my house, my house?" Mikey asked. His triple hop of happiness began. He was smiling with his whole body. The mailman was walking toward our house with his head down, looking in his mail bag, and Mikey asked him, "What's your name? Name? Name?"

I wonder if I'll ever stop feeling embarrassed when he asks questions to total strangers. The mailman looked at him and kept walking toward the mail slot on our front door.

Mom stood up quickly from where she was sitting on the front stoop with me and began moving toward Mikey. She said, "Mikey, this is our new mailman. He'll bring us our mail every day."

The mailman just looked at Mom. I wouldn't describe his look as friendly. I guess you could say I'm pretty good at reading the looks on people's faces. It was a look that said he didn't want to stop and talk to Mikey or to Mom.

Just then, Mikey tried to touch the mailman's bag. "Mine! Mine! Mine!" Mikey said as he followed the mailman.

The mailman's look turned to annoyed, and he pulled his mail bag away and continued walking to the next house.

Mom was standing close enough to the mailman to say, "We just moved in, and my son really likes to meet new people and watch them do their jobs…"

"Well, he can watch, but he can't touch my mailbag," said the mailman.

Mom said something quickly to the mailman that I couldn't hear. He looked over at Mikey, looked back at Mom, and said bluntly, "OK. I have to go finish delivering mail now." Then he turned and walked away to the next house.

I'm glad that Mikey didn't notice the mailman's rudeness. He was just watching for the next person to drive down our street so he could ask them to beep their horn. At least he was quiet. I asked, "Mom, what did you say to the mailman?"

"I just told him that Mikey gets extra excited because he has autism," said Mom.

Sometimes I wish that Mom wouldn't tell everyone our family business. What if the mailman doesn't even know what autism is? I was trying to not feel mad at the way he wasn't friendly, but I barely had time to think about that because I was watching Mikey call, "Hi! Hi! Hi!" to someone in the distance.

Some Questions
(that don't have answers)

How can Mikey watch cars on our street for hours, but he can't sit through a TV show or a movie?

Why does Mikey like cars to beep their horns so much?

Why did Mom tell the mailman that Mikey has autism?

Chapter Seven
Gavin and Pam

"Hi! Hi! Hi!" Mikey yelled across our street to a lady. She was pushing a stroller with a little boy in it. The lady was sort of old—I thought maybe she was the boy's grandma. And the boy looked like he was too big to be sitting in a stroller. Neither one of them seemed to notice Mikey saying hi.

Mom glanced up from the newspaper. "Keep your feet on our grass, Mikey." That's how she reminds him to stay safe and not run into the street.

I noticed that there was something familiar about the grandma. She was across the street, so I couldn't see her that well, but there was something about her that I recognized. *How could she be someone I knew? We just moved here.*

"Hi! Hi! Hi!" Mikey called across the street to them again. Either the grandma couldn't hear him or she was ignoring Mikey. "Hi! Hi! Hi!" he yelled again. He never gives up. The boy in the stroller just looked up into the sky. He didn't notice Mikey either.

Then I remembered where I knew that lady from. "Hey, Mom, isn't that the rude lady from the grocery store today?"

Mom took a closer look at her. "Yes, Katie, I think you're right. It looks like her. But remember, once I explained to her that Mikey has autism and he was in his own world while looking at the chips, she wasn't rude."

"Well, now *she* is the one ignoring *him*!" I told her. Mikey was still at it, calling to her across the street.

"Maybe she really doesn't hear him, or maybe she's focusing on the boy in the stroller. He must be her grandson." Mom was always trying to get me to think more positively.

As I looked across the street, I could hear the lady saying, "No, Gavin. You have to stay in the stroller." Mikey loved watching this. For some strange reason, Mikey loves watching when other kids get into trouble.

Well, this little boy, Gavin, must have been strong because he unbuckled himself and hopped right out of the stroller! He ran clumsily into the street. Mom stood up quickly and ran toward the little boy to help. Luckily, no cars were coming. The grandma was not as fast as Mom. When Mom took the boy by the hand to lead him back to his grandma, he pulled Mom in the other direction. He led Mom over to the fire hydrant in between our front yard and Julie's yard. Gavin was interested in the fire hydrant.

The grandma finally made it across the street, pushing the empty stroller. She was out of breath. "Gavin! You can't run into the street like that!" she told him as she took him by the hand. Then she looked up at Mom and said, "Thank you for getting Gavin out of the street. He just loves these fire hydrants so much. I can't seem to keep him in his stroller when we walk by one." Mom was smiling at her. The lady looked over to Mikey and back at Mom. I could tell from how the look on her face changed that she recognized them too. "Oh, I met you at the grocery store today! What a coincidence that we live so close. I'm Pam."

"We just moved in." Mom introduced us all to Pam.

"This is my grandson, Gavin. I watch him some afternoons while his parents are at work," she said. "Say hello, Gavin."

He didn't say hello. He was making grunting sounds about the fire hydrant.

"OK, time to get back in your stroller so we can go home for lunch," Pam said as she smiled at Gavin. She really did seem nice. Gavin looked like he was in his own world. He didn't budge from his spot next to the fire hydrant even as Pam kept repeating that it was time to go. "Sometimes he has a hard time listening," Pam said. She sounded a little bit flustered.

"How old is he?" I asked.

"Almost three." Pam held up three fingers.

Mom helped Pam get Gavin away from the fire hydrant. She sang a soft song to him about getting in the stroller and eating lunch.

Once Gavin was buckled into his stroller, Pam said, "Wow, you're really good with kids. How did you get him to listen?"

"I sang a song about what he's going to do next."

"Well, thank you. I definitely needed your help," Pam said. "I couldn't get him back into the stroller by myself. He's just getting too big and too fast for me."

"I'm so glad I could help," Mom said.

"Bye! Bye! Bye!" Mikey said as Pam turned the stroller to walk away.

This time, Pam waved good-bye to Mikey as she said, "Bye, Mikey. I take Gavin on lots of walks, so we'll see you again soon."

"Time to go inside, Mikey. We need to get ready to go to the pool now," said Mom.

* * * * * *

Once we were inside, Mom asked me, "Did Gavin remind you of anyone?" She was getting our bag ready for the pool. Mikey was upstairs putting on his bathing suit. That's one of the things he can actually do on his own.

I thought for a minute. "No, not really. Why, does he remind you of someone?" I asked.

"Yes, he's very similar to Mikey. Especially when Mikey was that age."

"Mikey doesn't like fire hydrants. He likes garbage trucks and being the Neighborhood Watch," I told Mom.

"Yes, but when Mikey was three, he didn't talk yet, and he had a hard time understanding danger and following directions. Actually, he still does," Mom added, "Gavin reminds me a lot of Mikey when he was three."

I was surprised. "Are you saying that Gavin has autism?"

"Well, I'm not a doctor so I can't determine that," she said. "But I did notice that Gavin has some of the signs that are linked with autism."

"Really? Like what signs?"

"Not being able to talk or make eye contact are two of them."

"Oh, I did notice that he didn't talk to us at all. I just figured he couldn't talk yet because he's a baby."

"Well, Katie, he's not really a baby. He seemed like a baby because he was in a stroller. He's almost three. Most three-year-olds are able to say lots of words."

I thought of my cousin who'd just had her third birthday a month ago. She has long conversations with me about her dolls and her stuffed animals. Mom was right. Most three-year-old kids *can* talk.

"What do you mean by 'signs of autism'? Is there a list or something?" I asked her.

"Yes, there is," Mom said. "I can show it to you sometime."

Signs of Autism in Babies and Toddlers

o Lack of eye contact - not looking at you when being fed or not smiling when smiled at.

o Child does not respond to his or her name.

o Child does not point or wave goodbye - or use other gestures to communicate.

o Child has no spoken words by 16 months.

o Child does not make noises to get adult's attention.

o Child does not imitate your movements or facial expressions.

Chapter Eight
Lifeguard on Duty

The Fairview City Pool was a quick three-minute drive from our house. When we arrived, first we had to register to become members. This took a while because Mom had to sign papers and pay money to join the pool. Mikey is not good at waiting. For anything. He gets loud and acts like a two-year-old when he has to wait. Mom usually packs some of Mikey's favorite things to distract him when we're out and he has to wait for something. I know she did this for me, too when I was a little kid, but she still has to do this for Mikey even though he's eleven. In her pool bag she had his favorite books, some snacks, and a new video on her phone that one of our old neighbors sent for Mikey. The video was of our neighbor's son beeping his car horn over and over. Mikey loves beeping horn videos.

I really didn't want Mikey to embarrass me by lying on the concrete outside of the pool office. That's what he does when he has to wait. He lies on the ground and makes a lot of noise. He was sitting there saying, "Swim, swim, swim," and he was getting louder. I had to think of something quickly that would keep him quiet. All the people who were walking through the pool entrance were looking at him.

"Here, Mikey, do you want your cereal?" I asked as I took the bag of Cheerios out of Mom's pool bag. Mom was still busy registering us to become members of the pool.

He grabbed the bag from me, opened it, and began stuffing the cereal into his mouth. It was keeping him quiet, so I tried to just ignore how gross he looked while he put fistfuls of Cheerios into his mouth.

"Uh-oh," I heard, and looked down to see that Mikey had spilled the bag of cereal all over the ground. I never know if he does that by accident or on purpose. I tried to clean it up by picking up the pieces and putting them back in the bag. If we were at home, I never would have helped him clean up. But I wanted to keep him quiet, so I kept picking up the tiny pieces. While I was cleaning up his mess, he went into Mom's bag and found his water bottle. He opened it, took one sip, and then poured the rest of it onto the ground—all over the small cereal pieces I was picking up.

"Mikey, why did you do that?" I asked him. Mom looked over at us. She had a frustrated look on her face but didn't say anything. I know if it had been me who poured my water out, Mom would have been mad and told me it was a waste of water. But she just ignored Mikey.

"Oh no! Oh no! Oh no!" he said. But he was smiling, so he didn't seem too upset. He's really good at making a mess. And this time I knew he spilled the water on purpose. Probably to see if he would get a reaction from me or from Mom.

I was starting to sweat. Partly because it was so hot, but mostly because I knew Mikey was about to have a major meltdown.

"OK, our pool cards are ready," Mom said. "Let's go in and take a look around."

I sighed with relief as Mom took Mikey by the hand and tried to get him off the ground. I carried the pool bag with all of our stuff so she could use both hands to get Mikey up. It took some time, but once she told him there would be water slides and lifeguards, his favorites, Mikey stood up and walked through the pool entrance.

This pool in Fairview City was much bigger than the pool in our old town. There were two giant water slides and three different pools to swim in. I even saw a sign for a snack bar and a mini golf course!

"Let's put our bags and towels down here," said Mom as she pointed toward a small group of chairs. Then she took Mikey by the hand to walk toward one of the lifeguards. As I put the pool bag down and draped towels over three chairs, I could hear Mom introducing Mikey and herself to the lifeguard. "We're new to town and just joined the pool. Can you please tell us the pool rules?

I was beyond embarrassed. Aren't all pool rules the same? No running. No diving in shallow water. No pushing kids in the pool. I could have told Mikey the rules myself. But the lifeguard, whose name was Joe, told us the rules. Mikey was listening while doing his triple hop of happiness. He loves lifeguards. Having Joe talk to us was a big deal for Mikey. I liked how Joe was talking more to Mikey and not really to me. I think he assumed I knew the rules. I also liked that he talked to Mikey the way he would talk to any other kid Mikey's age. Sometimes people talk to Mikey the way they would talk to a baby, with a high-pitched and excited voice. I know Mikey acts younger than his age, but he's not a baby. That's for sure.

Joe finished explaining the pool rules to Mikey:

POOL RULES

WALK SAFELY (NO RUNNING)

NO DIVING

NO PUSHING

ONE AT A TIME ON THE WATER SLIDES

GO FEET FIRST DOWN WATER SLIDES

NO FOOD/DRINKS IN OR NEAR THE POOL

Mikey asked Joe about the lifeguard chairs and the schedule for when the lifeguards change from one chair to the next. Most people don't realize this, but lifeguards have to change to a different chair every twenty minutes. They also have to take a break once per hour. Mikey learned this from the lifeguards at our old pool in Connecticut. He had the entire schedule memorized and would always walk the lifeguards to their chairs when it was lifeguard change time. That's what he calls it—"Lifeguard Change Time"—as if it's a big event.

Joe told him the lifeguard chair numbers and explained the schedule for lifeguard change at the Fairview City Pool. Mikey tried to ask more of his annoying questions, but Mom interrupted with, "OK, Mikey, that's enough questions for Joe." Someone always has to remind Mikey when to stop asking questions or else he would keep going all day.

Joe took a step toward Mom and said softly, "I'm a special education teacher during the school year. I'm a lifeguard during the summer. I get it." He smiled at Mom and me.

I like how he said this so Mikey couldn't hear him. Not like it was a secret, but more so Mikey wouldn't feel different.

"Is it OK if I take a quick walk with Mike around the pool to show him all the lifeguard chairs?" He said this loud enough for Mikey to hear.

It was funny to hear Joe call him *Mike*. No one calls him that. Everyone calls him *Mikey* or *Michael*. But it was OK with me that Joe called him *Mike*. It made him sound older, which I liked.

While Mikey and Joe walked a lap around the pool, Mom said, "Are you going swimming, Katie?"

I love to swim, and I'm actually pretty good at it. But it felt strange being in a fun place like the pool without any friends. That's the part that stinks about moving. I had to start all over again.

While I was feeling a little sorry for myself, a woman put her pool bag on the chairs right next to us. She had two kids with her. Something about the mom was familiar.

Mikey and Joe returned from their walk, and he loudly announced, "Only seven more minutes till lifeguard change, Mommy!"

"OK, great, Mikey," Mom said. "Thanks for the walk, Joe. I guess we'll see you up in a chair soon?"

"Yup, in about seven minutes I'll be up in chair number four over there." He pointed to a lifeguard chair on the other side of the pool. "Mike knows where I'll be. See you later," Joe said as he walked away.

"Bye, Joe! Bye, Joe! Bye, Joe!" Mikey said. Then he asked, "How many more minutes, Mommy?" Even though he was the one who just told us it would be seven minutes, he was asking anyway. He always asks questions that he already knows the answers to.

"I'd say we are down to six minutes now, Mikey," she replied.

"Oh, hi, Mikey," said the mom who looked familiar to me, the one who put her pool bag on the chairs next to ours. Her kids were already swimming in the pool. *How does she know Mikey?* I wondered. "Hi, Anna. Hi, Katie."

Mom and I both smiled and said hello. I don't think Mom knew who she was either. We'd been meeting so many new people all at once that it was hard to remember everyone.

Mikey looked at her quickly and then looked away and asked Mom, "How many more minutes now?"

Mom put up five fingers to show five more minutes.

"I'm Sally. I met you earlier today when I was walking my dog, Lucky," she said. She took off her sunglasses, and now I recognized her.

I would have recognized her right away if she was with Lucky. Would she have known it was Mom and me sitting next to her if Mikey hadn't come back from his walk with Joe?

Sally's daughter came running out of the pool. "Mom, the water is freezing today. Where's my towel?"

Sally handed her a towel and said, "Ella, this is Katie and Mikey. They just moved in down the block."

"Hi," I said to Ella. She smiled through her chattering teeth and said hello back to me, but she was staring at Mikey. He was walking in circles, saying, "Four minutes, four minutes, four minutes."

Ella asked her mom, "Four minutes till what?"

"Hi, Ella. I'm Mikey and Katie's mom. You can call me Anna," Mom said. Ella said hello to Mom as she waited for her mom to answer her question.

I was waiting too, as I wondered how Sally was going to explain to Ella what Mikey was talking about.

"Mikey's counting down the minutes till the lifeguards change chairs," Mom explained. Ella had a confused look on her face, so Mom continued, "He likes to watch when lifeguards climb down from their chairs at the end of their shift."

"OK," Ella said, but she still sounded confused.

Mikey was walking in circles muttering, "Almost time, almost time, almost time." I saw Mom gently touch his back to get his attention. Then she pointed to where the lifeguards were gathering their towels and walking to their assigned chairs for lifeguard duty.

I heard Mikey's loud screech, "IT'S TIME! IT'S TIME! IT'S TIME!" He stopped walking in circles and started his triple hop of happiness.

I've learned that there's really no way to expect Mikey to be quiet at lifeguard change time. So I don't even try anymore. It's impossible to ignore him because he's so loud. I guess watching lifeguards change chairs is as exciting to Mikey as watching cars drive by on our street. Something I'll never understand. I sat down in a chair as far away from him as I could so it looked like I wasn't with him. That's what I try to do sometimes when I get embarrassed. I just pretend that I don't know him.

Mikey continued screaming, "Wow! Wow! Wow!" at the top of his lungs. At our old pool, this wasn't embarrassing because all the lifeguards knew Mikey and expected him to be loud. But here at our new pool, I could feel my stomach do a flip, and I knew my face was red. I could see Ella staring at Mikey. It made me think of the way I usually feel when friends come to my house for the first time.

Mikey held hands with the lifeguard who'd just stepped down from the lifeguard chair closest to where we were sitting and walked her over to the next chair. I noticed she had a smile on her face, so I guess she didn't mind. Mom let him go since it was close and she could watch him. "I guess he will make lots of new lifeguard friends today," Mom said, trying to make a joke. I rolled my eyes.

Ella was still staring at Mikey, but I noticed it was more of a curious and kind look than before, when she seemed confused by him. I really am good at reading people's expressions. "He must really love lifeguards," she observed.

"Yes, he does. Lifeguards and garbage men are his favorite people to watch," Mom said.

"That's cool," Ella said, and she sounded like she meant it. She was still staring at Mikey as he clumsily skipped and hopped back to where we were sitting. But her stare didn't bother me anymore. I could tell she was trying to understand Mikey.

"Mommy, Mommy, Mommy," Mikey said. "Did you see it? Did you see it? Did you see it?"

"Yes, Mikey, I saw it. That was an awesome lifeguard change!" Mom replied.

"How many more minutes?" he asked.

"Minutes till what?" Mom asked.

"Till the next lifeguard change," Mikey said.

"Well, Joe told us they change chairs every twenty minutes, so I would say we have about nineteen more minutes to wait," Mom told him.

I think for Mikey, nineteen minutes feels like two hours.

"Mom, I'm hungry," Ella told her mom. "Can we go up to the snack bar?"

"Sure. Do you want to show Katie and Mikey where it is?" Sally asked her.

Oh no, I hope Mikey doesn't want to go with us.

"Sure." She smiled at me. "Have you gone yet? They have the best ice cream and soft pretzels."

I didn't realize how hungry I was till she mentioned the food. "Mom, can I go?" I asked.

"Sure. Mikey do you want to get a snack too?"

"No, Mommy, I have to wait for the lifeguards. Sixteen minutes, sixteen minutes, sixteen minutes."

I was so relieved that he didn't want to go with us.

"OK, Katie, here's some money to buy yourself a snack." Mom handed me a few dollars.

"Thanks, Mom." Ella and I started walking up to the snack bar. I turned around to see if Mikey was going to follow us, but he was still staring at the lifeguards. *Phew!*

As we stood in line to pay for our ice cream, I noticed the girl working the cash register was our nice waitress from the pizza place yesterday. I saw her puzzle piece necklace and her nametag said Erin, so I knew it had to be her. As I paid, I smiled at her, and she smiled back, but I could tell she didn't recognize me. *I think people only know who I am if Mikey is with me.*

Ella and I sat down in the shade to eat our ice cream. She asked me why Mikey was so interested in lifeguards.

I told her, "Most kids who have autism have a

thing that they're really into. For Mikey, it's lifeguards and garbage trucks and being the Neighborhood Watch." I explained what that meant.

"I didn't know that kids with autism have a thing they're really into," she said. "I thought people who have autism can't talk." She looked confused.

"Some kids with autism *can* talk, like Mikey. He actually talks too much," I explained. "And others don't use words but communicate in different ways."

Ella said, "This may sound like a silly question, but what is autism again? I mean I know I've learned it before but…"

"It's not silly to ask. But it can be hard to explain," I began. "Autism makes it hard for a person to deal with the world around them. Some people with autism have trouble communicating and understanding what people think and feel." I continued, "Usually, people with autism need a specific routine to feel safe. Mikey sort of needs that. Most people with autism have interests that are very different from kids their age."

"My brother is really into hockey. That's his thing," Ella said.

I nodded. *I wish my brother was into hockey instead of being into lifeguard schedules, garbage trucks and being the Neighborhood Watch.*

"And he's really annoying," she added. We smiled at each other, in agreement that brothers are annoying.

What Mikey Loves

Lifeguards

Garbage and recycling trucks

Routines

Being The Neighborhood Watch

Memorizing the school lunch menu for the month

Chapter Nine

I Scream, You Scream,
We All Scream for Ice Cream

That evening after dinner, we sat outside. Mikey was the Neighborhood Watch as Mom and I sat on the uncomfortable front stoop. We'd given up on sitting in the back yard. Some of the neighbors who live on our street were getting used to seeing Mikey outside, and they actually beeped their horns for him as they drove by. Mikey screamed, "Again! Again! Again!" every time a car horn beeped for him.

Julie beeped as she slowed her car down to turn into her driveway. Mikey ran toward Julie's car as she and Caroline were getting out of it. He began asking his usual questions: "Where were you? Are you going out again? What time will you be back?" He never waits for the answers. He just asks question after question.

"Hi, Mikey. I was just driving Caroline home from her play practice," Julie said. I liked how she chose just one of his questions to answer. The one that actually made sense for him to ask.

Mikey was close enough to Julie to grab her phone out of her hand, but instead he grabbed her car keys. "Lock your doors, lock your doors, lock your doors," he told her as he pushed the buttons on her keys.

Of course he pushed the red panic button on the keys and made the car alarm go off. He was smiling from ear to ear. Mom darted off the stoop and dashed over to take Julie's keys out of his hand. She pushed the button to stop the loud sound of the alarm and handed the keys back to Julie.

"Mikey, put your hands in your pockets," she told him in a firm tone. She thinks this will stop Mikey from grabbing things. But I know it won't.

Caroline walked over to me, "Hi, Katie, what's up?"

"We joined the pool today, "I told her.

"Oh cool. Did you go on the slides?"

"Yes, they were awesome."

"Did you try the ice cream?"

"Yup!"

"Maybe we can go to the pool together tomorrow."

"That would be awesome," I told her. "Do you know a girl our age named Ella? I met her today at the pool."

"I know Ella. She lives on the next block," Caroline told me. "She has a really cool dog named Lucky."

"Yes! I met Lucky yesterday. He's so cute," I replied.

"I love dogs, but my parents won't let us get one," Caroline told me.

"Same here," I told her.

I heard music playing in the distance. Caroline heard it too—I could tell because her eyes lit up and she asked, "Mom, can I have money for the ice cream truck?"

Of all the new sounds in our neighborhood, the ice cream truck music was going to be my new favorite. It was getting louder, which I knew meant that the truck was getting closer.

Julie searched in her purse for a few dollars and handed them to Caroline, who said, "Thanks, Mom!"

I looked at Mom with my best "please look." Even though I already had ice cream at the pool, I was hoping Mom would let me get something too.

Dad was walking down our block, on his way home from the train station. Now that we live in New

York, he takes the train to work. "Daddy! Daddy! Daddy!" Mikey screamed, as if it was the first time he'd seen him in a year. He ran over to give him a giant hug.

Dad gave Mom and me our hugs too. Then, he grinned and asked, "Is that music what I hope it is?" Dad LOVES ice cream.

"If you hope it's an ice cream truck, then yes," I told him.

His smile got even bigger. Sometimes he acts like a kid. Especially when ice cream is involved. He put his hand in his pocket and pulled out some money. "OK, we're ready, Katie." He winked at me.

By now the ice cream truck was on our block. I don't know who was more excited, Mikey or Dad. Mikey doesn't even like ice cream, but he loves watching people order food.

The ice cream man stopped his truck right in front of our house. Caroline and I ordered first. A few younger kids from our neighborhood ordered next. Mikey loves to place orders, so when it was Dad's turn, he told Mikey to order an ice cream sandwich for him.

Mikey looked at the pictures of the different ice cream options on the side of the truck and said, "Ice cream sandwich please, ice cream sandwich please, ice cream sandwich please."

The ice cream truck man looked at Dad and said, "Can I help you?"

Dad said, "Yes, my son was ordering for me."

Mikey repeated, "Ice cream sandwich please." Three times of course.

"What's he saying? I don't know what he said," the ice cream man said impatiently.

Mikey talks too fast when he's excited. He's hard to understand sometimes, but especially when he's excited.

"Mikey, slow down, and say it loud and proud," Dad said.

"Ice. Cream. Sandwich. Please," Mikey said. He was loud.

The ice cream man made a face that looked like he was annoyed and handed Dad his ice cream. "Thank you, thank you, thank you," Mikey said. But the ice cream man was already taking an order from the next kid in line.

When the ice cream man didn't reply, Mikey said, "Say 'You're welcome.'" No reply from the ice cream man again. This is something that really bothers Mikey. He knows the automatic response *you're welcome* comes after *thank you*. Just like *bless you* comes after a sneeze. He learned all the responses in speech therapy over the years. I could feel a meltdown starting.

The ice cream man was busy helping other customers. He really didn't seem to care about my brother and the fact that he needed a *you're welcome* in that moment.

Mikey threw himself to the ground. The tears were starting, and he was screaming, "Say it, say it, say it," to the ice cream man. All the people standing in line to buy ice cream were staring at him.

Mom knelt down and sang a soft song to him about going inside to call Nana. That's his biggest treat—calling Nana and Papa on the phone. He loves talking to them and could easily talk to them for hours. He seemed to forget about the missing *you're welcome* and ran inside to find the phone.

"Catastrophe avoided," Dad said as he took a bite of his ice cream.

"What do you mean?" I asked. "What's a catastrophe?"

"A catastrophe is a disaster," Dad explained. "We almost had a meltdown disaster over a missing *you're welcome*."

"Oh, I get it. The phone call to Nana saved the day."

"Bingo," Dad said as he started walking toward the front door. "Katie, I'm going inside to see if Mom needs help with Mikey." I nodded and gave him the thumbs up sign since my mouth was full of ice cream.

Caroline was still outside too. "Look, Katie, here comes Ella and her mom with Lucky."

I looked down the block. Sure enough, Sally and Ella were coming for ice cream and walking Lucky. Caroline and I walked over to say hello to them and pet Lucky. Lucky licked my hand, and I tried to keep my ice cream away from him as I scratched behind his ears. *Oh my gosh, Lucky only has three legs!* He looked and acted like a regular dog. But he only had three legs. I wondered why. *What happened?* I think my hand was frozen in stillness on Lucky's head.

Sally must have noticed that I had stopped petting Lucky because she asked, "Oh, did you notice about Lucky's missing leg? That's why we call him Lucky."

What's lucky about having three legs instead of four? I know I had a very confused look on my face.

"He was hit by a car when he was a puppy," Ella said.

"One of his legs had to be removed after the accident," Sally continued. "We didn't know if he would be able to walk again, but he's still able to do everything he did when he had four legs. He walks, he runs, he plays fetch, and he gives us the best doggie love and kisses."

"Wow, that's amazing!" I didn't know what else to say, so I just smiled at Sally.

"Some people notice Lucky's missing leg right away. And others don't see it at first," Sally continued.

It made me think of Mikey. I always wondered if people noticed right away about his autism. About how different he is. Or if some people don't see that at first.

Ella was at the ice cream truck getting her ice cream. When she came back, she let Lucky have a lick of it.

The ice cream truck drove away and turned the music back on. It was getting dark, so I said good-bye to Caroline, Ella, and Sally. I gave Lucky a pat on his head and walked through our front door to go inside for the night.

Lucky

I didn't notice his missing
leg at first

He is able to do what other
dogs do - take walks, play
fetch, give doggie love,
and everything else

I wonder if some people
don't notice Mikey's
autism at first just like I
didn't notice Lucky's
missing leg at first

Chapter Ten
Old Friends

There's a time each evening just after Mom puts Mikey to bed when the house is finally quiet. It's the only time of day that our house feels calm. I love this time of day. I know it's odd that my older brother goes to bed *earlier* than I do, but Mom says he needs extra sleep.

I was in my room looking through an old photo album when Mom knocked on my door. She'd just finished putting Mikey to bed. "You've done a great job getting your room unpacked and organized," she told me.

"Thanks," I said as she sat on my bed.

"What do you want to do tomorrow afternoon? In the morning, we're going to get back-to-school haircuts," Mom said.

Oh no, was she kidding? I didn't want to get my

hair cut. I like my hair long. Plus, I didn't even want to think about school—we still had a few weeks left of summer before school started. "Mom, do I have to go?" I asked. "I don't even need a haircut."

"Well, Mikey does. I found a barber who knows how to cut hair for kids who have autism," Mom said. "I looked it up online."

Mom was always looking on the computer for places that were "autism friendly." Places like restaurants, movie theaters, barbers, and other public businesses that said they understood the needs of kids with autism.

"Mom, I really don't want to go to an autism-friendly barber. Can I please stay home alone?" I asked.

"No, Katie."

"Why not?"

"Because you're not old enough," Mom replied.

"But you've let me stay home alone before," I reminded her.

"I have?" Mom asked. "When?"

"When we lived in Connecticut. Every time you went to help Mikey with his garbage jobs on our street, you would leave me home alone," I reminded her. "I like staying home alone."

"That's different, Katie. I was just walking in our

85

neighborhood to make sure he was safe while pulling out the neighbors' garbage cans. I wasn't going out in the car."

"But you were gone for a while," I pleaded. "I can do it."

Just then, Mom's phone buzzed. She glanced at the screen. "Katie, you're saved by this text from Julie. She and Caroline have invited you to go to the pool with them tomorrow. You don't have to come to the barber with Mikey and me."

"Catastrophe avoided," I said.

"Ha! Good one! Where did you learn that?"

"From Dad." I smiled. "I really didn't want to go and watch Mikey get his haircut," I said, feeling relieved. "Do you think he'll be good?"

"Who, Mikey or the barber?" Mom laughed.

"The barber, Mom." I rolled my eyes. "Do you really think he'll know what to do?"

"Well, the website says that this barber shop is autism friendly, so I hope so," Mom said.

"What does that even mean?" I asked. "Does it mean the barber is friendly to kids who have autism?"

"It means he can cut hair for kids who are extra wiggly or nervous and that he welcomes kids with autism into his shop," she explained.

"So how does this barber know how to keep kids calm and still?" I wondered.

"Maybe he took a special class about how to cut hair for kids who have autism or other disabilities."

"They have classes like that for barbers?" I asked.

"Yes, I think so," Mom replied. "Or maybe he has his own child or a relative or neighbor with autism. Those are the people who really get it or want to get it," Mom said.

"I guess the mailman and the ice cream man don't know anyone with autism. They *really* don't get it," I said.

"I was thinking the same thing, Katie. But"—she had a hopeful look on her face—"maybe they'll end up learning something from our family."

"What do you mean?" I asked.

"Well, you've done this before. Last year at school, you, Lauren, and Bella realized that some of your classmates just did not get it about autism. You figured out just how to teach them so they'd understand it better."

I smiled at Mom and then looked over at my bulletin board. I could see the picture of Lauren, Bella, and me that was taken on the day we did our first presentation about disabilities for our classmates. That was really one of the best things I've ever done. "It was like *we* were the teachers. We made that PowerPoint presentation, and all the teachers wanted us to come to their classrooms," I said.

Mom said, "Yes, well, you are a—"

"Little big sister," I interrupted.

"That's true. You are definitely Mikey's little big sister. But I was going to say you're an expert on what it's like living with someone who has a disability," Mom said. "That's why your presentation was so great."

"What will the mailman and the ice cream man learn from our family?" I asked.

"They have a lot to learn, don't they?" Mom asked.

As I nodded to agree with Mom, I heard my iPad buzz on my desk. It was a FaceTime call from Lauren! "Mom, it's Lauren! I know it's late, but can I talk to her?"

"Yes!" Mom sounded as excited as I was about Lauren calling.

I tapped "accept call" and saw Lauren's and Bella's faces on my screen. "Hi, guys!" I said.

"Katie!" they both squealed. Then they saw Mom behind me and said hello to her.

"Hi, girls! So nice to see your smiles. We miss you!" Mom said.

"We miss you too!" they said together through their happy giggles.

"OK, I'll leave you girls alone so you can catch up," Mom said. She left my room and as she was closing the door she gestured for me to be quiet so that Mikey wouldn't wake up."

"How's New York?" asked Lauren.

"It's OK," I said.

"Do you have good neighbors?" Bella asked me.

"They can't be as great as her *old* neighbors." Lauren smiled.

We all laughed together. It felt good to laugh with old friends. "What's new there?" I asked.

"We miss you," Bella said.

"It's boring here without you," Lauren added. Bella nodded in agreement.

"Have you met any new friends yet?" Bella asked.

"My neighbor, Caroline, is really nice. You guys would like her," I said.

"How's Mikey?" asked Lauren. "Tell him we miss him!"

"He's good. He likes the Fairview City Pool, and he's only gotten lost once so far. But we found him right next door," I told them.

"Can we say hello to him?" Bella asked.

"He's sleeping already," I told them.

"Oh yeah, I forgot how early he goes to bed," Bella replied.

"Katie, you have chocolate on your mouth," Lauren pointed on her own mouth where my chocolate evidence was.

I used the back of my hand to wipe the chocolate off my mouth. "Oh, that's from a treat I got tonight from the ice cream truck."

"Lucky! You have the ice cream truck in your new neighborhood? That's awesome. I wish the ice cream truck would come here."

"Well, eating the ice cream was awesome," I told them. "But..." I hesitated because I didn't know how to describe the ice cream man.

"But what?" Lauren asked.

"The ice cream man was sort of rude to Mikey," I told them.

I explained how the ice cream man was impatient with Mikey and wouldn't say *you're welcome*. Then I told them about the mailman and how he seemed to not really get it about autism either. They both nodded, as if they understood how I was feeling. It felt good to tell my friends what was on my mind.

"Sounds like you have your work cut out for you," Lauren said.

"What do you mean?" I asked.

"Well, don't you want the ice cream man and the mailman to get it about Mikey?"

"Yes."

"So how are you going to teach them?" she asked me. Lauren had a way of challenging me to think about the things I didn't really want to think about. But I knew deep down that they were the things I should be thinking about.

"I don't think I can sit them down and have them watch our presentation from last year."

"No, you'll have to do something different, that's for sure," Bella said.

"Like what?" I asked.

"We will think of something," Bella said.

"*We?*" I asked. "You guys will help me?"

"Of course, Katie. We're a team!" said Lauren. "Just because we live far away now doesn't mean we can't help with this kind of stuff."

"Yup, we're friends forever," Bella added with her huge smile.

I have the greatest friends in the world. They gave me that awesome feeling in my heart. I think it's called hope.

Lauren and Bella

They totally get it about
Mikey

They are the greatest friends

They are good listeners

I miss them

We are a good team because
we help each other when we
need help

Chapter Eleven
A Hopeful and Helpful Day

Mom says that I'm usually grumpy in the mornings, but today I'm not. I woke up with a hopeful feeling in my heart and a smile on my face. Maybe it was my late-night chat with my old friends that was putting me in a good mood. Or maybe I was looking forward to hanging out with Caroline at the pool today. I got dressed quickly and went downstairs to eat my breakfast. I walked into the kitchen just as Mikey took the last bite of his eggs. Perfect timing.

As he got up from the table to run to the front window to be the Neighborhood Watch, Mom stopped him. "Time for your special drink," she said, holding the small red cup of medication.

"Stand still, and it won't spill. Stand still, and it won't spill. Stand still, and it won't spill." Mikey sort of sang it like a cheerleader. "Right, Mommy? Now you say it, Mommy!"

"Good morning, Katie," Mom said as I slid into my chair at the kitchen table. "Did you sleep well?"

"Say it. Say it. Say it," Mikey demanded. It's almost impossible for me to have a conversation with Mom when he's in the room.

I tried to answer Mom's question quickly before she was distracted by Mikey again. "Yes, I slept in. I stayed up late talking to Bella and Lauren last night."

"Say it. Say it. Say it!" Mikey demanded even louder.

Mom looked stuck. She needed Mikey to take his medication. But I know she wanted to listen to me. "Stand still, and it won't spill," Mom said. I rolled my eyes.

"Good job, Mommy!" Mikey said, and then he drank his special drink in one quick sip and ran out of the room to be the Neighborhood Watch. Even though I was frustrated, I laughed when Mom gave me a funny look after Mikey told her she'd done a good job. It was pretty funny to hear a kid say that to his mom. I don't think Mikey was trying to be funny, though. I think he just repeats what other people say to him.

"Remember, today you're going to the pool with Caroline and her mom," Mom said.

"Uh-huh," I replied since my mouth was full of cereal. *Of course I remembered. I couldn't wait!*

"I packed a pool bag for you with extra towels, sunscreen and some money for lunch. Please pack your goggles and a water bottle," Mom reminded me.

"OK, Mom, I will," I said. "What time am I going to the pool with them?"

"Caroline's mom said to go next door at around 10:30, which is perfect because I'll be leaving then with Mikey for his haircut. He and I will meet you at the pool after lunch."

At 10:30, I said good-bye to Mom and Mikey. I walked over to Caroline's house and saw she was already outside with her mom in the driveway, packing the car with their pool bags. "Hi," I said.

"Hi, Katie," Julie said. "We're so glad you can come to the pool with us. Caroline doesn't like going alone. She says the pool's no fun without a friend."

Same here!

"Mom, are we ready to go, or do we have to wait for Nick and Tommy?" Caroline asked as we climbed into the backseat of Julie's car. I hadn't met Caroline's brothers yet.

"We're ready. Your brothers are staying home and doing their summer reading homework." She turned to me and explained, "In middle and high school, you have to read a few books for school over the summer, and the boys haven't even started their books yet." "It doesn't look like they're doing much reading, Mom. I think they're still sleeping," Caroline said.

"I know, I'm letting them sleep in first. They know they have to read a few chapters before I pick them up for the pool," Julie explained as she began to back out of the driveway.

This was so different for me. I couldn't even imagine being able to leave my brother at home alone.

From the backseat of Julie's car with my window open, I heard Mikey yelling, "Beep, beep, beep!" to Julie. He was jumping up and down in our front yard. At least he was staying in our yard today instead of wandering into Julie's back yard.

Julie beeped her horn a lot, which made Mikey smile with his whole body. "Thank you, thank you, thank you." He may be annoying, but he's always polite!

Julie opened her window and said, "You're welcome!"

Then Caroline shouted, "See you later, Mikey!"

They've only known us for a short time, but it felt like Julie and Caroline really "got it" about Mikey.

When we arrived at the pool, Julie said, "would you like me to drop you girls off at the front entrance while I go park the car? Then I'll meet you inside at our usual spot in five minutes."

Caroline and I looked at each other with huge smiles. "OK, Mom," Caroline said.

"Then you can practice walking in by yourselves," Julie told us. "Caroline, your brothers were a little bit older than you are now when I began allowing them to ride their bikes to the pool on their own."

Even though Mikey was the same age as Caroline's brother Tommy, I couldn't imagine Mikey ever going to the pool alone. But I *could* imagine doing it myself. Caroline and I got out of the car and walked through the entrance, showing our pool membership cards. We walked to the chairs where her mom said to meet up. I loved feeling so independent.

After we sprayed ourselves with sunscreen, Julie arrived and sat down to read her book. I've *never* seen Mom read a book at the pool. She's usually chasing Mikey around. Caroline and I walked over to the giant slides. They were the kind of slides that you see at water parks, with tunnels and twists. At the top of the giant staircase there's a platform that leads to the two slides. We had to wait in a short line.

A pool attendant was up at the top next to the two slides. I could tell he worked at the pool because he wore a shirt that said "STAFF" on the back. It looked like his job was to tell the kids waiting in line when it was safe to go down the slides.

The boys ahead of us in the line were trying to go down the slide together, and the pool attendant yelled at them, "ONE AT A TIME!" His voice was so loud that I jumped a little bit. Next I heard him yell, "FEET FIRST!" to another boy who was trying to go down head first.

When it was finally our turn to go, I knew to go feet first and one at a time. I didn't want to get yelled at by the pool attendant. But he yelled, "GO! What are you waiting for?" at Caroline and me. He sounded mad. *Why was he yelling at us? We didn't do anything wrong.*

We went down the slide a few more times even though the pool attendant was always yelling the rules. On our fourth trip up the stairs, a new attendant with the staff shirt was climbing up in front of us. When she got to the top she said, "OK, David, time for your break."

The grumpy slide attendant said, *"Finally,"* in his grouchy voice and walked down the stairs.

Caroline and I waited our turn, and when we got to the front of the line, the new pool attendant said, "Ready, girls?" We nodded. "Have fun," we heard her say as we started down the slides.

What a difference! She was so much nicer. I decided to stay away from the slide when David was working.

Caroline and I were getting hungry, so we stopped to say hello to her mom and get our towels and money for the snack bar. On our way to the snack bar, we passed by the kiddie pool. I noticed Pam pushing Gavin's stroller. He was wiggling and fidgeting with the buckle of the stroller, trying to get out. I heard Pam say, "No, Gavin, Grandma can't chase you in the water right now. We have to set up our towels on some chairs and put on sunscreen first."

I could tell that Gavin wasn't going to be able to wait for his grandma. Of course he wanted to go in the pool. I turned to Caroline. She was watching Gavin and his grandma, too.

At the same time, we said to each other, "Let's take Gavin in the kiddie pool." Then we both laughed!

I walked up to Pam and Gavin. I said, "Hi, Gavin, I'm Katie. Remember me?" He stared straight ahead. He didn't look at me even though I had bent down to be eye level with him. I took my sunglasses off my face and pushed them up on my head. I thought maybe he just didn't recognize me with my sunglasses on.

I shook my head to make my sunglasses fall off my head. I had a feeling that would get Gavin's attention. As they fell to the ground, Gavin looked at me. I had his attention! I put the sunglasses back on top of my head and made them fall off on purpose by moving my head. He looked at me again. Immediately, I made the sunglasses fall off my head again, and this time Gavin smiled! He almost looked like he was going to laugh!

I looked up at Pam. She looked happy. "Hi, Katie. It's good to see you here," she said. "Hi, Caroline. I'm so glad you girls have become friends since you're neighbors."

By this time, Caroline and I were both putting our sunglasses on our heads and making them fall off to get Gavin to smile. "Can Gavin play with us in the pool?" I asked.

Silence. She was probably wondering if we could handle him. "The kiddie pool, not the big pool of course," I added.

"I don't know. He's fast, and he likes to run away," she said. "Are you girls sure? It would be a big help to a tired grandma like me!"

"Yes!" we both said at the same time again.

"OK. Thank you," Pam said.

I looked at Gavin. He was still trying to get unbuckled from his stroller. I reached down to help him. As soon as the seatbelt was unbuckled, he took off for the kiddie pool. Pam was right—he *was* fast! I had to move quickly to keep up with him. I tried to get his attention by calling his name. He didn't look at me. He seemed to be in his own world. Now that he was out of the stroller and on the move, our sunglasses game wasn't working to get his attention anymore.

Caroline and I just followed Gavin around the kiddie pool, making sure he stayed safe. There were mini slides to climb and a giant mushroom that looked like an umbrella with water streaming down. I could tell that Gavin loved the water, but he never looked at us or smiled. It was like he didn't even realize we wanted to play with him.

I thought about how Mom explains to our new babysitters how to get Mikey's attention. She tells them that when Mikey acts like he is ignoring them, they have to get close to him. She tells them to put a hand gently on his shoulder or forearm and say, "Look at my face, Mikey." Usually having the babysitter be close helps Mikey look at her (or him) and listen. Then the babysitter can give the directions (like "time for bed" or "let's go get a snack").

I decided to try it. I went over to Gavin and put my hand on his shoulder. He stopped moving. I knelt down so my face was next to his face. I said, "Gavin, please look at my face." It worked! He looked at me. I had that good feeling in my heart. I smiled, hoping he would smile back. He didn't smile, but I could tell he was listening. "You're a great swimmer." That's all I could think of to say in that moment. He stayed still. He really looked at me. He almost smiled at me. I could see it in his eyes. Then he went back to the kiddie pool slides. Back to his own world.

I saw someone jumping up and down on the other side of the kiddie pool. At first I thought it was a little kid, but when I looked closer I realized it was Mikey— he looked a little bit different with his haircut. It was lifeguard change time, so I knew he would be jumping until that was over. I spotted Mom a few feet away from Mikey, talking to Pam. Mom waved at me, and I waved back. I went back to checking on Gavin with Caroline. He was sitting and splashing in the shallow water.

Pam held up a bag of Goldfish crackers and called Gavin's name. He didn't look up. I used Mom's strategy again. I put my hand on his shoulder, and put my face close to his face. "Gavin, look at my face," I said. It worked again! He looked right at me. "Your grandma has Goldfish for you. Look," I said, pointing my finger to where Pam was standing with the bag of crackers.

Gavin grunted, and then his eyes looked where my finger was pointing. "Mmmm, mmmm," Gavin said, and he quickly began running through the shallow kiddie pool over toward Pam.

Caroline and I followed Gavin out of the pool. Pam handed him the bag of Goldfish and dried him off with a towel. Gavin put a fistful in his mouth. "These are his favorite crackers," Pam said. "You girls were wonderful with him in the pool. Thank you!"

"You're welcome. We had fun," I told Pam.

"I'm glad Katie and Caroline could help you," Mom said to Pam. "Hi, girls. You must be hungry for lunch."

"Yeah, we're starving," I said.

"Why don't you go up to the snack bar now and meet Mikey and me down by the pool when you're done," Mom said.

* * * * * *

Caroline and I ordered our lunch at the snack bar. Erin was the cashier again. She said hello to Caroline and

103

asked me, "Aren't you Mikey's sister?"

I nodded. I was so happy she recognized me without Mikey.

"Is he here today?" Erin asked me.

"Yeah, he'll be up here for a snack with my mom later."

"OK, good. I hope to see him," Erin said.

Caroline and I paid for our burgers and fries, said good-bye to Erin, and found an outdoor table where we sat down to eat. As I took the first bite of my burger, I heard a loud voice yelling, "NO RUNNING." It was David again—the grumpy attendant from the pool slide was now working at the walkway that leads to the snack bar. Some boys around our age were running to the ice cream cart and getting yelled at by David.

"I guess he likes yelling at kids. He's really good at it," Caroline joked.

"He was so rude to us on the slide," I said. "I don't want to go anymore when he's the one working at the slides."

"It looks like he works in lots of different places at the pool," Caroline said. "We can't avoid him."

I knew Caroline was right. Since this guy worked at the pool, we would see him all over. Not just at the slides. I was nervous because I knew he would yell at Mikey—that's why I wanted to avoid him. I could tell he didn't get it at all.

Gavin

*He loves the pool, fire
hydrants and goldfish
crackers*

*I think he understands
what I say to him*

*He spends a lot of time with
his grandma, Pam*

He can run fast

*I wonder when he will
learn to talk*

Chapter Twelve
Family Day at Adventureland

It was our first weekend in the new house. Mom had read in the local newspaper that Adventureland, an amusement park just thirty minutes away, was having a sensory-friendly day for kids with autism. I could hear Mom and Dad discussing it over breakfast as I was coming down the stairs.

"I think we should try it," Dad said. "It'll be fun. Mikey loves rides, and so does Katie."

"I don't know. We've had so many new things this week," Mom said. "New house, new town, new everything. I don't know if Mikey can handle another new thing."

I love rides, especially water rides. I really wanted to go! As I walked into the kitchen, I asked, "What are you guys talking about?" I didn't want them to know I'd overheard them talking about Adventureland.

"We're deciding if we should try out Adventureland today," Dad said. "Here, look at the pictures of the rides." Dad turned his laptop screen so I could see the Adventureland website.

The rides looked awesome! "Can we go? Please! I want to go on this ride!" I said as I pointed to a fun-looking roller coaster. It was called the Scream Chaser.

"I don't know if Mikey can handle so many new things in one week," Mom said.

"Why does it always have to be all about Mikey?" I asked.

"Let's just try it," Dad said. "If it doesn't work out, it's only thirty minutes away, and we can get back home quickly." I could tell he was trying to convince Mom. Dad loves rides too, so I knew he wanted to go!

Mom was sitting at the table, writing a list. She's a list person, like me. "What are you writing, Mom?" I asked.

"I'm making a list of all the things we need to pack for Adventureland," she said. "Sunscreen, bathing suits, a change of clothes, towels. Can you think of anything else?"

Dad and I smiled at each other. "So we're going?" I asked.

"You and Dad are good at convincing me." She smiled at me. "Plus, I want to go on that roller coaster too." She pointed at the Scream Chaser.

"Thanks, Mom!" I said as I hugged her.

"We should leave soon, though. The later it gets, the more crowded Adventureland will be, and you know how Mikey is around big crowds," she reminded us.

That made me think of the time we tried to go to the beach last summer. Mikey wanted to go to the pool, but Mom and Dad insisted it was a beach day. It was so crowded at the beach that we barely had a spot on the sand to put our towels down. Mikey kept throwing sand and dumping out his water bottle instead of drinking it. Since the beach was so crowded and unfamiliar to him, he didn't like it. We had to leave early. He ruined the beach day. I hope he doesn't ruin today.

Dad called Mikey into the kitchen and showed him the pictures of Adventureland on his laptop. "Does that look like fun, Mikey?" he asked.

"Fun! Fun! Fun!" Mikey said.

"We're going there today," Mom told him.

Mikey looked at her. "Rides today? Rides today? Rides today?" he asked.

"Yes." Mom pulled out the piece of paper where she had written down a schedule for Mikey. Mikey loves reading schedules, so Mom usually writes things down for him. That way he knows what's coming next. She started reading the schedule to Mikey. It sounded like a little song the way she read it to him. Mom says Mikey listens better when music is involved.

Adventureland Schedule

- [ ] Drive to Adventureland
- [ ]
- [ ] Wait in a line to buy tickets
- [ ]
- [ ] Put sunscreen on
- [ ]
- [ ] Go on rides
- [ ]
- [ ] Eat lunch
- [ ]
- [ ] Go on more rides
- [ ]
- [ ] Drive home
- [ ]

Mikey started jumping up and down and flapping his hands. He was smiling with his whole body. I guess he liked the schedule.

The car ride to Adventureland went by quickly. Just like Mom's schedule said, we stood in a line to get our tickets. While we waited, we put on our sunscreen. When we got to the ticket window to pay, they had to put bracelets on our wrists. I knew Mikey would pull his bracelet off, but they put one on him anyway. I noticed that Mikey's bracelet was blue, while the rest of ours were white.

Dad looked at the Adventureland map, and we followed him to our first ride, the Scream Chaser. Now that we were here and I saw how tall the roller coaster tracks were, I could feel the butterflies in my stomach, but I knew I wanted to try it.

The attendant at the beginning of the long line for the Scream Chaser said to Mom, "You can wait in the sensory-friendly line," and pointed to a much shorter line.

"Oh, thank you," Mom said.

I asked Mom how the attendant knew we needed the sensory-friendly line. I always wonder if people can tell that Mikey has autism from just looking at him. But Mom said that the attendant noticed Mikey's blue wristband and that's why she directed us to the sensory-friendly line. That's one good thing about having a brother with autism. You get to wait on shorter lines at amusement parks.

There were two families ahead of ours in the sensory-friendly line. The boy at the front of the line was in a wheelchair. He was about my age. I noticed his wristband was also blue. His dad was helping him out of the wheelchair and onto the ride. He reminded me of Bella. He needed help to walk, but he had a huge smile on his face.

The next family had a boy a few years younger than me who was wearing headphones. They were the kind of headphones that don't plug into anything but help to keep things quiet. Mikey used to have those, but he doesn't really use them now. Loud noises don't bother him so much anymore, but some kids with autism can't handle loud noises. I checked the headphone-wearing boy's wrist, and his bracelet was blue. He was crying, saying, "Me turn." I could tell his mom was trying to distract him by showing him pictures and videos on her phone.

Then our family was next in line. Mikey gets tired really easily and doesn't like to stand for a long time. He loves the hot sun, so he moved to lie down in a patch of sun while we were waiting. If we were in the regular line, I would have been so embarrassed that my brother was laying on the ground. He looked like he was sunbathing. But in the sensory-friendly line, lying down on the ground wasn't embarrassing. I was just glad he wasn't screaming.

It was our turn to get on the Scream Chaser. Mikey sat with Dad, and I sat with Mom. I was nervous, but I put on my brave face.

The coaster slowly climbed up the first big hill. I could see all of Adventureland from up here. I tried not to look down. The first downhill drop was terrifying, but the rest of the ride was so much fun. I was glad I challenged myself to ride the Scream Chaser.

"Again! Again! Again!" Mikey yelled when the ride was over. He loved it. I did too, but I didn't want to go on it again. Mom and I stepped out of our Scream Chaser seats.

"Would he like to ride it again?" the ride attendant asked Mom. "Guests wearing blue bracelets can ride twice without getting off."

Mom looked down at Mikey. He and Dad were still strapped into their roller coaster seats. "Mikey, would you like to ride again?"

"Go! Go! Go!" he said.

"Have fun, buddy!" the attendant said. "But when you come back after this ride, you have to get off."

I liked the way the attendant talked to Mikey. His voice was patient, but he didn't sound like he was talking to a baby. It bothers me so much when I hear people do that.

Mom and I waited by the exit of the Scream Chaser while Dad and Mikey rode it again.

When they got back, Mikey yelled, "Again! Again! Again!"

The attendant told him he had to get off. "Remember, buddy. I told you it's time to get off. Other kids are waiting. You can come back later if you want."

I thought Mikey was going to have a meltdown since he wasn't getting what he wanted. Surprisingly, he got off the ride and hopped to the exit, where Mom and I were waiting.

"More rides? More rides? More rides?" Mikey asked.

"Do you guys want to go on the bumper cars or Free Fall next?" Dad asked as he checked the Adventureland map.

"Bumper cars! Bumper cars! Bumper cars!" Mikey said. I loved the bumper cars too, so I was glad he chose that next. I was finally tall enough to drive my own car! So was Mikey, but Dad shared a car with him. He would never figure out how to drive it safely on his own. Every time Dad and Mikey bumped me, I saw Mikey flap and heard him say, "More! More! More!"

It felt good to be able to do fun things together as a family. We usually have to divide into two groups. One kid with one adult. But this day at Adventureland was working out for us to be together.

During lunch, Dad finished eating first and offered to go to the locker to get our sunscreen and towels. We were heading to the water rides next. As soon as Dad left, Mikey announced that he had to go to the bathroom.

Since Dad was at the locker getting our stuff, he couldn't take Mikey to the men's room. "OK, Mikey. We all need to change into our bathing suits anyway," Mom said. "Let's go find a bathroom." I knew we needed to find a family bathroom. The family bathroom is usually for parents changing a baby's diaper. But for us, the family bathroom is a place where Mom can bring Mikey to a public bathroom and help him if he needs it.

I had my eye out for a family bathroom, but I didn't see one. I was about to ask someone, but I heard Mikey repeat, "Mommy, pee now, pee now, pee now," and he was starting to pull his shorts down. Mom was holding both of his hands now to keep him from pulling off his shorts while she walked quickly to the entrance of the ladies' room. We had to go to the closest bathroom now which happened to be a ladies' room instead of a family bathroom so that Mikey wouldn't have an accident. I started to slow down so it didn't look like I was with them.

"C'mon, Katie. You can't wait out here alone," Mom said. I didn't move. "You need to change into your bathing suit, so just come in and get that done while I'm in here with Mikey," she said.

It was beyond embarrassing. I mean, it's OK when you see little boys who are about two or three years old in the ladies' bathroom with their moms. But when boys are as old as Mikey, it's just strange.

Mom had to go into the stall with Mikey to help him change into his bathing suit. At home, he can change into it himself since he sits on the ground. Mikey loses his balance easily, so he needs to sit while changing into his clothes. But in a public place, he needs Mom's help to change since he can't sit on a dirty public bathroom floor while changing. I was a few stalls over getting changed and was done way before they came out of their stall. Mikey was being so loud, asking Mom his usual questions like, "Mommy, what are you having for breakfast tomorrow?" and "Mommy, are you having a sensational Saturday?" Everyone could hear him, and I wanted to disappear.

Once Mom was done helping him get changed, the door to their stall opened, and she walked him over to the sinks. Mom told Mikey to wash his hands. She saw

I was quietly waiting by the exit, and she gestured for me to keep an eye on him while she went back into the stall. As soon as Mikey was done washing his hands, he looked around for Mom. In a worried voice, he said, "Mommy? Mommy? Mommy? Where are you?" That's another embarrassing thing—when your eleven-year-old brother calls your mom *Mommy* instead of *Mom*.

Mom said, "I'll be right out, Mikey." *Good, I didn't have to say anything.*

"Where are you, Mommy? Are you in the bathroom?" Mikey asked. His voice was full of fear. "I don't see you, Mommy."

"Yes, Mikey, I'll be right out. Please go stand next to Katie and wait for me." *Oh no! Now all the people in the bathroom would know I'm related to the boy in the ladies' room.*

"Mommy, are you going number one or number two?"

Mom didn't answer, but I heard some of the other moms in the bathroom laugh at his question. I always wonder if they're laughing at him or if they just think he's funny.

"Mommy, are you going number one or number two?" Of course he asked it again. He needed his answer. More laughing from almost everyone in the bathroom.

Just at that moment, Mom opened the bathroom stall door. "Mikey, time for water rides," she said. Her face was a little bit red. It takes a lot to embarrass Mom, but this was one of those times.

I knew Mom would have a talk with Mikey on the drive home about appropriate and inappropriate questions. Specifically, how asking people if they are going number one or number two is an inappropriate question. I have heard her tell him this about three hundred times in my life, which did not give me much hope about him ever stopping.

Dad met back up with us after the bathroom incident, and we had a fun afternoon on the giant water slides and lazy river.

* * * * * *

It was time to go home. On our walk out of Adventureland, we stopped at a snack cart to buy water and a snack for the car ride home. Mikey still had his blue bracelet on, and I noticed that the man selling snacks wore a blue shirt with a puzzle piece on it.

"Four waters! Four waters! Four waters!" Mikey said to the man selling snacks.

"Hi!" the man said to Mikey. "Four waters coming right up." He turned around and reached into a cooler for the water bottles. "Can I get you anything else, buddy?" he asked Mikey.

"Chips! Chips! Chips!" Mikey said as he pointed to the yellow bag of potato chips.

The man put the chips on the counter next to the waters.

"What's your name? Name? Name?" Mikey asked.

"I'm Mike," the guy said. Then he pointed to his name tag. "See my name tag? It says my name."

"Mikey, Mikey, Mikey!" he said and pointed to himself. Mikey was jumping and flapping and could barely see because he was smiling so big that his eyes looked almost closed!

The guy understood right away. "Wow, we have the same name? Fist-bump me!"

After we paid, Mikey said, "Thank you, thank you, thank you!"

Snack Bar Mike said, "You're welcome, Mikey. Come back soon!"

As we walked to the car, I had a smile on my face. Mike from the snack bar had been so good with Mikey. It made me wish that the ice cream man and mailman could get it like Snack Bar Mike did.

Thankful

That our family got to do
something fun together,
all 4 of us

For fun rides at Adventureland

For strangers who just seem to
get it, like Mike, who sells the
snacks at Adventureland

Chapter Thirteen
A Great Idea

Sitting out on the front stoop was becoming our evening routine. Lots of people were out riding bikes and walking dogs. It was so different from our old neighborhood in Connecticut. Here in New York, if I walk outside the front door, everyone can see me right away since the houses are so close together and so close to the street. In Connecticut, if I took a step outside the door of my old house, no one would know but me.

Mom and Dad were sitting on the stoop, and Mikey was wandering on the grass, closer to the sidewalk. Mom said, "Mikey, keep your feet on our grass." I was practicing my cartwheels on our front lawn.

I could see Pam walking down the sidewalk toward our house with Gavin in his stroller. There was another person with them, pushing Gavin's stroller. "Mom, look, here comes Gavin," I said. "Who is that lady pushing his stroller?"

"Oh, good. That must be Pam's daughter. She's Gavin's mom. I've been wanting to meet her," Mom said as she stood up to wave at them. Pam and her daughter waved back.

"Hey, Katie, is that the little boy you've been helping out with at the pool?" Dad asked me.

"Yes, his name is Gavin," I told Dad.

"I've heard that you've been a huge help to his grandma," Dad remarked. That made me smile.

Pam, Gavin, and his mom were now only a house away on the sidewalk, so I could hear what they were saying.

"This is the family I was telling you about," Pam said to Gavin's mom as she gestured toward our house. "The family with the daughter who plays with Gavin at the pool." She paused and then realized I was right there because I walked over to them and said hello to Gavin. At first it seemed like he was ignoring me, but then I bent down to his eye level and gently touched his arm. He looked right at me! I think he remembered me, I could see it in his eyes.

"Hi, Katie!" Pam said. "This is Gavin's mom, Meredith."

"Hi," I said, and smiled at them both.

"Katie! I am so glad to meet you!" Meredith said. "Gavin's grandma keeps telling me what a big help you are with him, especially at the pool. And now I see why she can't stop talking about you. You're so great with him!"

I didn't know what to say, so I just smiled at her and said, "Thanks." My parents came over to meet Meredith, and I started playing with Gavin. I didn't have my sunglasses, so instead I used a small toy from his stroller tray and played the game we invented at the pool.

Mikey walked over to watch us play "toy-on-my-head" and said, "Again, Katie! Again, Katie! Again, Katie!" Mikey was laughing like he'd heard the funniest joke in the world just from watching the toy fall off my head. I wish I could laugh that hard about something so simple. Gavin was watching Mikey laugh.

As the adults talked, I stayed close partly because I wanted to play toy-on-my-head with Gavin but mostly because I wanted to hear what they were saying.

"Anna, I think you told me that you have a book and some papers for Meredith to read," Pam said.

"Yes, I do! Grant, please keep an eye on Mikey while I run inside to get something," Mom said to Dad.

"Sure," Dad said.

When Mom came back out the front door a minute later, she had a folder in her hand and a smile on her face. "Meredith, you should call this number first to make an appointment," I heard Mom say as she pointed to one of the papers in the folder. "They'll come to your house and help you get started." Mom sounded like she really knew what she was talking about.

"Gavin's doctor gave me the same phone number," Meredith said. "I guess I've been putting it off, hoping Gavin would start talking on his own."

"I know what you mean," Mom said. "It's hard to make the first call, but once you do, Gavin will get the help he needs. A speech therapist will come to your house to help him learn to talk."

I was listening to Mom and Meredith, and I guess I stopped the game of toy-on-my-head for a few seconds. Then I heard Gavin grunt, "Mmm, mmm."

"Did you hear that?" Meredith asked. "I think Gavin was asking you for 'more,' Katie! He really responds to you."

I put the toy on my head. Mom, Pam, and Meredith watched me and then looked at Gavin. I know they were all hoping he would say "mmm" again. He didn't, but he smiled when I let the toy drop to the ground.

I leaned into Gavin, touched his hand lightly, and said, "Do you want more, Gavin?"

He started flapping and said, "Mmm, mmm, mmm." He really reminded me of Mikey in that moment.

"Look! He almost talked again!" Meredith said. It looked like she had tears in her eyes. She looked at Mom and said, "Thank you for the book and this folder. I'll make the call on Monday about getting speech therapy for Gavin." Mom and Meredith hugged.

I played toy-on-my-head a few more times while Mom talked to Pam and Meredith. Dad was walking with Mikey on the sidewalk. They were standing in front of the streetlight.

"Bye, Katie, it was so nice to meet you," Meredith said to me as she and Pam left, pushing Gavin in his stroller to continue their evening walk.

"Bye!" I said. "Gavin, I hope I can play with you again soon," I told him.

He didn't look at me or wave good-bye. But he flapped when he heard me say his name. And I know he enjoyed playing the toy-on-my-head game.

Meredith and Pam noticed the flap too and smiled at each other. "Yes, Katie. I'll let your mom know next time we're going to the pool. Maybe you can meet us there and help me with Gavin again," Pam said. "You were such a huge help to me last time we saw you there."

"OK," I said. I never realized that just splashing around with him was so helpful. I was just having fun with him.

After they left, I asked Mom, "What was in that folder you gave to Meredith?"

"Oh, that's just some information about how to get help for young kids who show signs of having special needs," Mom told me.

"What kind of help?" I asked.

"Well, kids Gavin's age who aren't talking yet can get speech therapy at their house," she told me. "That helped Mikey a lot when he was Gavin's age."

I nodded. "Was there anything else in the folder?"

"Just some information that was helpful to me when Mikey was Gavin's age. And a book that helped me understand about Mikey's different ways of learning."

That gave me an idea. I couldn't wait to call Bella and Lauren to tell them about it.

I heard a loud screech and immediately knew it was Mikey. "It's on! It's on! It's on!" he screamed with joy in his voice. He was jumping up and down because the streetlight in front of our house had just turned on.

Most boys his age cheer like that when their favorite football team wins the Super Bowl. Mikey gets excited over a streetlight turning on at dusk.

I looked around and noticed a few neighbors were outside. They must be getting used to Mikey's loud noises because none of them were staring at him.

Mikey was standing there, hugging the lamppost and staring up at the streetlight with a huge smile on his face. I walked over and tried to talk to him. I wanted to see if his happiness was contagious. Could he get me to feel happy about the streetlight too? He was mesmerized by the light. In his own world. There was no way he'd even realize I was there to talk to him.

As I was standing with Mikey, Caroline and her mom drove into their driveway. She had been at her cousin's house all day and then at her final play practice.

"Hi, Katie," Caroline said as she got out of her mom's car. "Do you think you can come to my play? It's tomorrow night."

"Yup, my mom already bought tickets for us to go," I told her.

"Oh, she did? Cool!"

"How was your cousin's party?" I asked her.

"It was good. They have a pool in their back yard, so we just swam all day." She paused. "My cousin has

126

a neighbor named Matt who reminds me of Mikey. I never really understood about autism until you became our neighbors. I didn't know that kids with autism can talk and play and are even fun to be around. Usually when we go to my cousin's house, I feel sort of nervous around Matt. But this time I played with him and felt totally comfortable around him."

"Wow, that's cool," I said. I was glad she told me. Just then, I heard the ice cream truck music getting closer to our block.

Mikey let go of the streetlight and began running toward the corner with Dad chasing after him. "Ice cream truck! Ice cream truck! Ice cream truck!"

The ice cream man stopped his truck right in front of our house again. Mikey went right up to him and ordered potato chips. I know, a bag of potato chips is an odd item to order from an ice cream truck, but Mikey doesn't like freezing-cold foods in his mouth.

The ice cream man gave Mikey the chips, and Mikey gave him his money and then ran away, saying, "Thank you, thank you, thank you." I knew he was hoping for a *you're welcome*, but the ice cream man didn't say anything.

Caroline and I were next in line to order our ice cream. "I'll have an ice cream sandwich, please." I looked over and saw Mikey standing on our front stoop with Mom and Dad. Mom was hugging him; he looked upset. As the ice cream man handed me my ice cream, I bravely said, "Can you please say 'you're welcome' to my brother? He has autism, and he really likes when people say 'you're welcome' after he says 'thank you.'"

What happened next I still can't believe. The ice cream man said, "That kid?" and pointed at Mikey. "No way, he doesn't have autism. He can talk. I've heard that kid talk. People with autism can't talk."

I stood there with my mouth hanging open. The ice cream man, who obviously knew nothing about autism, just told me that my own brother didn't have autism. Dad was walking toward me with some money in his hand to pay for my ice cream. He must have heard the whole thing because he said, "Many people with autism can talk. My son, for example."

"Oh, I didn't know that," the ice cream man said.

You have a lot to learn, I was thinking.

"I'm dealing with kids all day, and sometimes they're rude. It's hard for me to tell the difference between rude kids and kids that have problems. Like your son."

"Well, my son doesn't have *problems*. He has autism," Dad said.

Caroline ordered, and when she thanked him, the ice cream man said, "You're welcome." Then he yelled out to Mikey, "Hey, kid!" Mikey actually turned around. "You're welcome!"

Mikey smiled with his whole body. I saw the ice cream man smile, so I told him, "My brother also likes when people beep their horns."

A few more neighbors bought ice cream. When the line of customers was gone, the ice cream man started his truck and began to drive away. He beeped his horn for Mikey!

Caroline looked at me and said, "Well, I guess you and Mikey are teaching the ice cream man just like you're teaching me."

I nodded. "Do you want to hang out for a while?" I asked her.

"I do, but my mom wants me to go to bed early because I have my play tomorrow. I'm supposed to get a good night's sleep," she said.

"OK. Well, see you tomorrow at the play!"

When I got inside, I wanted to FaceTime my old friend, Lauren right away. When I saw her face on the screen, I told her about my idea. "I saw my Mom give a folder to Gavin's mom, and it gave me an idea," I told her.

"I'm all ears," she said.

"I was thinking I could make a folder or something

with information about autism to give to the people who just don't get it. People like the ice cream man and the mailman."

"You know what? I think that'll work." Lauren paused. "But instead of a big folder, maybe we can do something smaller," she suggested.

"Like what?" I asked her.

"Well, just yesterday some people rang my doorbell asking for a donation for a walk they're having to raise money for childhood diabetes," she started.

"Did you give them any money?" I asked.

"Yes, I gave them some of the money I saved from last time we had a lemonade stand. They gave me a card called *All About Diabetes* with information that most people don't know about diabetes in children. I learned a lot from it."

"What do you mean, like a birthday card?" I asked.

"No, more like the size of a business card. Let me get it to show you," she said.

Lauren held up the *All About Diabetes* card so I could see it on my screen. It fit right into the palm of my hand. I knew that's what we had to do! But our card would be an *All About Autism* card. I couldn't wait to tell Bella. And Caroline too!

<u>Mikey Is Helping People Get It about Autism</u>

Caroline said she felt more
comfortable around
another boy with autism
all because she knows Mikey

The ice cream man finally
said you're welcome to
Mikey and beeped his horn

I wonder if more people will
understand about autism
better because of Mikey

Chapter Fourteen
Caroline's Play and Unexpected News

Dad came home from work early so that he could watch Mikey while Mom and I went to Caroline's play. Before we left, Mom gave Mikey his special drink. "Stand still, and it won't spill," she told him as usual.

"Good job, Mikey! Good job, Mikey! Good job, Mikey!" he said after he drank the medication. Sometimes he says the words that he thinks others will say to him.

Then Mom repeated, "Yes, good job, Mikey!"

Mom and I stopped at the pizza place for a quick dinner before the play. I was hoping to see Erin working there, but we had a different server tonight. I was happy to have Mom all to myself. Usually in restaurants she has to sit next to Mikey and barely has time to talk to me since she's making sure he doesn't bolt out of his chair or do anything else unpredictable.

One time in a restaurant, as we were walking to our table, he grabbed a handful of French fries off a customer's plate. We were so embarrassed, but luckily the person just laughed. Ever since that happened, Mom and Dad tell him to walk with his hands in his pockets when he's in restaurants.

Tonight it was just Mom and me, so we could actually have a calm conversation without worrying if Mikey would grab food off someone's plate. As we ate our pizza, she asked me if I had talked to Lauren or Bella recently.

"Actually, I talked to Lauren last night," I told her.

"How is she doing?" Mom asked. "I'm sure she misses you."

"Yeah, but we didn't talk about that," I told her.

"What did you guys talk about?" she asked as she took a bite of her pizza.

"Well, we are planning to make business cards," I told her.

"What business are you starting?" She seemed very interested.

"We're not starting a business. We're making cards with information about autism that will help people who just don't get it."

"I like this idea," she said. "Tell me more!"

"Remember that day at the grocery store when we met Pam?" I asked Mom in between bites of pizza. "I could have given her a card about autism then."

"Oh, I get it," Mom said. "The mailman should read your card about autism."

"Yup. I remember you telling me that we can't really expect people who don't live with autism to understand. This will be my way of trying to help them get it."

"Wow, Katie, that sounds like a great idea," Mom said. "You have the best ideas about how to help people really get it about autism. First the presentation at school last year, and now this."

"After watching you give Gavin's mom the folder last night, it got me thinking about giving something to people who don't get it. Like the ice cream man and the mailman."

"Yes, definitely the ice cream man!" Mom laughed. "Although he did a little better last night, didn't he?"

"Yeah, he did. After Dad and I talked to him," I said. "Anyway, Lauren suggested we make something smaller than a folder. So we are creating All About Autism cards."

"That's a great name, Katie. What information are you going to put on the cards?" Mom asked.

"We still have to decide, but probably facts about autism. Stuff that most people just don't know."

Mom took a sip of her water and motioned with her hand for our waitress to bring the check. "If you need any help, let me know. But I'm sure you girls want to work on this yourselves."

As we left the pizza place and walked to the car to go to Caroline's play, Mom's phone rang. It was Dad. She put the phone to her ear. "Yes, I already gave him his special drink before I left," she said to Dad. Then she said, "No, Mikey, you can't wait outside for the streetlight to go on. It's time for bed now." I guess Mikey grabbed the phone from Dad's hand and that's why she was talking to him now. The call ended quickly, though, because Mikey always pushes the end call button even before the phone call is over.

We got to the high school auditorium and found our seats. I was reading the program to see if I could find Caroline's name when someone began speaking into the microphone on the stage.

"Welcome to our summer play! We have a treat for you. Tonight we have a performance before the play. Please welcome the members of our Unified Theater program to the stage as they perform some of their favorite songs and scenes from the Disney movie *Frozen*."

A group of kids around my age and a little bit older walked onto the stage. They began singing, and I realized many of the kids had special needs. When you live with someone who has special needs, you can pick that out pretty quickly in others. I also saw Erin up on stage holding hands with a girl who had Down syndrome. Now I knew why she wasn't working at the pizza place tonight. I quickly read my program and found the description for Unified Theater. It said:

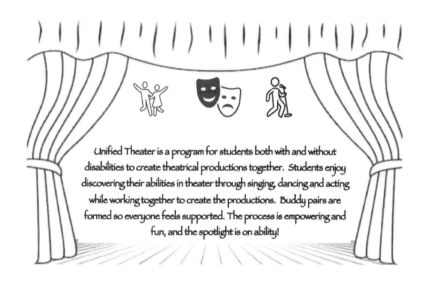

Unified Theater is a program for students both with and without disabilities to create theatrical productions together. Students enjoy discovering their abilities in theater through singing, dancing and acting while working together to create the productions. Buddy pairs are formed so everyone feels supported. The process is empowering and fun, and the spotlight is on ability!

That's cool, I thought. "Mikey would love being a part of this. Maybe he can do it next summer," Mom whispered to me during the performance. I was thinking the same thing.

The Unified Theater group got a huge round of applause and a standing ovation at the end of their performance. There was a short break before Caroline's play started.

* * * * * *

Caroline has a great singing voice. I didn't know that about her! She even had a solo. She is so brave to get on stage and sing in front of a huge audience. I don't think I could ever do that. But then again, I didn't think I could do a presentation in front of my class last year, and I did that.

When the play ended, we waited to see Caroline so I could give her the flowers we brought for her. "Caroline, that was awesome! You're such a great singer!" I told her.

"Thanks, Katie! I'm so glad you could come to the show!" Caroline gave me a hug.

She was still in her costume and stage makeup so she looked older. Julie invited Mom and me to get frozen yogurt with them to celebrate. I went in Caroline's car, and Mom met us there. While the four of us were sitting together eating frozen yogurt, Mom got another phone call from Dad.

"I have to take this call." She excused herself and

walked outside to have some privacy. She came right back in, and I noticed her face looked different. Not sad, not happy, just different. She said, "Julie, can you take Katie home when you're done here? I have to go right now."

Julie nodded. "Sure, is everything all right?" she asked.

"No. Mikey just had a seizure." I could tell she was trying to keep her voice steady. "I have to get home right away." Then she looked at me. "Katie, I don't want you to worry. I'm sure Mikey is fine. I just need to go help Dad." Then she ran out to the car.

How was I supposed to not worry? That was impossible. I couldn't take another bite of my frozen yogurt. I tried hard not to cry. Julie said, "Katie why don't you come to our house until your mom has this figured out, OK?"

I know she was trying to help, but I still didn't feel any better. I nodded, still holding my breath, trying to hold back tears. Even though Mikey was the most annoying brother ever and always embarrasses me, I don't want him to have seizures. I want him to be OK.

When we got home, Dad was outside waiting for me. He hugged me tighter and longer than usual. He thanked Julie and told her and Caroline that Mikey was going to be OK. They went back to their house. Our house was so quiet when Dad and I went inside. He told me that Mom had talked to Mikey's doctor on the phone even though it was late at night. Since Mikey's seizure lasted less than three minutes, the doctor said he didn't have to go to the hospital tonight.

"Dad, are you sure Mikey is OK?" I asked. "I don't want him to die," I said. The tears I'd been holding back came quickly.

Dad hugged me. "I know this seems scary, Katie," he said in a very quiet and calm voice. "Mikey has epilepsy. He is not going to die from this. We're lucky to have found a medication that works for him to not have seizures for so many years. Mom will take him to the doctor tomorrow to find out what is going on." He took a deep breath, put his hands on my shoulders, and looked into my eyes. "Maybe he needs a new medication now that he is getting bigger. He is almost a teenager."

"What if he has another seizure tonight?" I asked.

"Mom's going to sleep in his room with him tonight to make sure that doesn't happen," Dad said. That made me feel a little bit better.

Seizures

I hope Mikey doesn't have
another seizure ever again

I wish Mikey could tell me
what a seizure feels like

I hope Mikey doesn't feel
pain or get hurt from his
seizures

Chapter Fifteen
Erin

The next morning, Mom had to take Mikey to the doctor for his seizure appointment. She asked Julie to keep an eye on me, but Julie had to take her boys to their back-to-school doctor appointments. Dad couldn't stay home from work because he had an important meeting. So she called Erin to babysit.

"Turns out Julie knows Erin's family and had her number. I sent her a text message this morning, and she'll be here in about fifteen minutes to hang out with you while I take Mikey to his appointment," Mom said.

I can't wait till I'm old enough to stay home alone. But I have to admit, usually I really like the babysitters who come over. When Mikey and I were younger, Mom said she would hire two babysitters to come together, so one could watch Mikey and the other could watch me. She said Mikey always needs someone watching his every move because he doesn't understand safety and never sits still.

One time, I remember, Mikey locked his bedroom door so that he and I, along with our babysitter, Paige, were all locked in his room. Luckily, Paige had her phone in her pocket so she could call Mom to let her know we were trapped. Mom was getting in her car to drive home and set us free when Paige figured out how to use a toy model of the Empire State Building that Mikey had in his room to pick the lock and get us out of his room. Mom always called Paige a genius after that. Mom told me that was the night she realized we needed two babysitters when we were younger.

Erin rang the doorbell. Mikey ran to the door with Mom right behind him. He was trying to unlock the front door. Sometimes, it's hard for him to use his hands to open small things like locks on doors. Mom calls it "fine motor control" and says that's why he goes to OT, which means occupational therapy. Mom began to unlock the door by turning the small knob halfway. Then she took a step back so Mikey was able to unlock it the rest of the way by himself.

When Mikey got the door open and saw Erin standing there, he was so excited to see her he smiled with his whole body.

"Hi, Erin, come on in," Mom greeted her.

Erin smiled. "Hi, Mikey," she said.

"Erin, Erin, Erin!" Mikey said. He always gives a warm welcome to babysitters.

"Hi, Katie," Erin said. "I'm glad we get to hang out today."

"Me too," I told her.

Mikey went back to using his iPad while Mom showed Erin around. I heard her say, "Erin, I usually give a training to our new babysitters telling them all about Mikey. He's a challenging kid to watch." She continued, "But for today, since you'll be with Katie, no training is required."

"OK," Erin said. "Katie and I will have fun together. I brought some of my string so we can make bracelets."

I noticed a pretty bracelet on Erin's wrist. I hoped she would teach me how to make one like that.

"You have my number if you need anything," Mom said to Erin.

"Yes, thanks," Erin told her.

Mom started making a snack bag for Mikey like she always does when he goes out. Then she told him it was time to go.

"No, Mommy. I want Erin, Erin, Erin!" Mikey said.

"Mikey, you go with your Mom now, and when you get home we can play, OK?" Erin said.

"No, no, no!" Mikey said. "Play now, play now, play now!"

"I have an idea," Mom said. "Erin, can you please send Mikey an email in about an hour? Here's his email address." She handed Erin a piece of paper where she had just written down his email address.

"Sure, I can do that." Erin smiled at Mikey.

"Then you'll have something to look forward to when we get home from the appointment," Mom said to Mikey.

Mikey smiled with his whole body again. He loves emails, and now he will have a new email friend to send messages to.

"Mikey, we can drive past the garbage trucks on our way to Dr. Levy's office," Mom said. That got Mikey out the door quickly. He loves seeing garbage trucks almost as much as receiving emails. "Bye, Katie." Mom gave me a quick hug and whispered, "He will be OK," in my ear. She knew how upset I was about the seizure last night. "Bye, Erin." She waved as she ran out the door to make sure Mikey was getting in the car and not running out to the street.

"Have you had breakfast yet?" Erin asked.

"No. I was going to have a bagel," I told her. "Do you want one?"

"Sure, I haven't eaten yet either. I was out late last night," she said.

"That's right, I saw you at the Unified Theater show!" I said. "That was really cool to watch."

"It's so much fun. You should try it next summer," Erin said. "You would be good at it," she added.

Wow, her kind words made me feel really good. "What do you do at Unified Theater?"

"We hang out, sing songs, and act out scenes from favorite movies," she explained. "This year, the theme was *Frozen* since so many kids love that movie and the music from it."

"How old do you have to be to join?" I asked.

"I think you can be any age," Erin said. "There were some girls there around your age. They try to have two partners for each kid there who has disabilities."

"How did you get interested in it?" I asked.

"I have a cousin who has autism. She's eight years old." Erin smiled as she told me about her cousin. "She doesn't live in New York, but I get to visit her in Massachusetts a few times a year. She reminds me of Mikey because she's really friendly. But my cousin doesn't talk with words. She uses a talker," Erin said. I could tell Erin really loved her cousin from the way her face looked when she talked about her.

"I know a kid from my old school who uses a talker too." As I told her this, an image of Adam's face popped into my head.

Erin continued, "I was eight years old when my cousin Emily was born. I loved having a baby cousin. Babies are so cute, right?" I nodded. "When she was two, she was diagnosed with autism. I was ten years old by then." She paused, and her face changed as if she was remembering something sad. "I remember my mom and her sister, Emily's mom, were very upset about autism at first."

I nodded as I took a bite of my bagel.

Erin continued, "So I made it my mission to find out as much as I could about how kids my age can help. That's when I found the Unified Theater website. I lucked out because there was already a Unified Theater program right here in Fairview City."

"I really hope Mikey and I will be in Unified Theater next summer!"

"Yes! You'll both love it," Erin said. "I started doing Unified Theater when I was ten. Then, when I turned eleven, I became a peer partner at Unified Sports."

"Does your cousin do Unified Theater or Unified Sports in her town?" I asked.

"Yeah, she does both. And she sings the songs for her performances with her talker," Erin answered. "My mom and I always go to her shows."

We finished our bagels, and Erin brought our plates to the sink. She was really easy to talk to and hang out with. "Do you want to make bracelets?" she asked.

"Sure," I said. "Did you make the one you're wearing?" I pointed to her wrist.

"I did. Do you like it?" she asked.

"I love it!" I told her. "Can you really teach me how to make one like that? It looks hard."

"It's easier than it looks," Erin told me. She got out her bag of string and told me to choose four colors. She tied my strings together and showed me how to get the bracelet started. It was sort of like tying knots. I watched Erin's fingers move and tie the strings, as she explained how to know when to make the knots that formed the bracelet. She was right, it was easier than I thought it would be.

Once Erin felt that I had the hang of it, she stopped coaching me on how to make the bracelet and started making one of her own. "What are Mikey's favorite colors?" she asked. "I'll make one for him while you're making yours."

"Green," I told her.

Erin pulled out four strings—all were different shades of green—and started on Mikey's bracelet.

"You know how before you said you made it your mission to find out how kids can help," I said. "When you found out about your cousin," I added.

"Yes," she answered.

"Well, I was wondering if you know of anything else besides the Unified Theater and Unified Sports," I said.

"At school, I'm in a club called Best Buddies," Erin told me.

"What's Best Buddies?" I asked.

"It's a really fun club where you get matched up with a buddy who has special needs or disabilities. Then, you and your buddy get to do fun things together both in school and on weekends," she explained.

"That sounds like fun," I replied.

"Yeah, it's a lot of fun. Oh, I can't believe I haven't mentioned my favorite event yet! The annual autism walk," Erin said. "See the shirt I'm wearing right now?" She pointed to her shirt as the bracelet strings hung from her hand. "It's from the walk last year."

She was wearing a blue shirt that said, "Shine a Light on Autism." Under those words, it said, "Walking to Spread Autism Awareness," with the year of the walk. She turned around, and I saw "Team Emily" on the back. Now I got it!

"Why is the walk your favorite event?" I asked.

"It's so much fun! We get our family and friends together, and we raise money to donate to local programs like Unified Theater, Unified Sports, and Best Buddies. We get a face painter and a magician, and some food trucks come." I could feel her enthusiasm for the walk. "It's a really fun day. The police close off the streets, so it sort of feels like a parade."

"When is it?" I asked.

"Soon, at the end of the summer. Labor Day weekend," she said.

"I'll tell my mom about it," I told her.

"Yes, your family should definitely be a part of the walk!"

"Is it one of those long walks?" I asked. I was thinking about the three-mile run that Mom and I did last year. Three miles was a lot longer than I'd thought.

"No, it's short so that everyone can participate. My cousin doesn't like walking long distances. She gets tired easily. So when my mom first organized the walk five years ago, we decided to make it begin and end at a playground. We just walk through the main street of Fairview City and back to the playground. At the end is when we have the face painter, the magician, and the food."

I told Erin about our experience with the ice cream man and the mailman in our neighborhood. She was a good listener and made me feel better after I told her.

Then I told Erin about my idea for the All About Autism cards to help people who don't get it yet about autism. She loved it and asked if I thought the cards would be ready by Labor Day for this year's walk.

"Oh, do you think we can hand out the cards at the walk?" I asked her.

"Definitely," Erin replied. "In fact, your card idea is giving me another idea of something else we can have at the walk this year."

"What is it?" I asked.

"You know those magnets that people put on the back of their cars?" Erin asked.

I nodded. "My dad has one for his favorite football team, and my mom has one for her favorite coffee shop."

"I know people will buy those at the walk." She started thinking out loud, sharing her ideas for what the magnets should say. She'd already decided the magnets would be in the shape of a puzzle piece.

I guess I better get started on making the All About Autism cards. Hopefully tonight I can call Lauren and Bella to get all our ideas collected into one list.

Erin

Her cousin has autism, so
she really gets it

Showed me how to make
cool string bracelets

She told me all about
Unified Sports, Unified
Theater and Best Buddies

I wish I had a big sister
just like her

I can't wait to go to the
Autism Walk that she told
me about

Chapter Sixteen
Mikey is OK

By the time Mom and Mikey got home from his appointment, I had already made three bracelets! I couldn't wait to show Mom.

Mikey barged through the back door and went straight for his iPad. "Did you send me my email, email, email?" he asked Erin as he stared at his iPad screen.

"Yes, of course!" Erin told him. "Did you get it?" she asked.

Mikey was scrolling through his emails and screeched "Erin!" when he saw her name. I guess he got it.

"Look what I made," I showed Mom the bracelet on my wrist and held the other two in my hands.

"Wow, Katie, those are fabulous!" Mom said as she

put her arm around my shoulder. "How was everything here?" she looked at Erin.

"It was great! Katie is the little sister I wish I had!" Erin told her. "Is it OK if I go hang out with Mikey for a little while?" Erin asked.

"Of course, that would be really helpful," Mom said.

"So what happened?" I asked Mom. She had a confused look on her face, almost like she didn't know what I was talking about. "At the doctor," I explained. I couldn't stop thinking about seizures and worrying about Mikey.

"Good news! Dr. Levy said Mikey had a seizure because he has grown so much taller in the past year," Mom told me. "He weighs more, so he needs more medication."

"Good news? Why is that good news?" I asked.

"Well, it's good that we know the reason for the seizure. Mikey needs more medication. When kids grow a lot, like Mikey did in the past six months, they weigh more. When you gain weight, you need more medicine," she explained.

This time I was the one with a confused look on my face.

"Katie, remember when you were six and started having allergies in the springtime?" Mom asked.

I nodded. I couldn't stop sneezing, and my eyes were so itchy. "Back then you only needed one purple chewy tablet for your allergies because you were smaller. Now that you're nine, you're bigger and stronger, and you weigh more than you did when you were six. So now you need two tablets. It's like that but with Mikey's seizure medicine."

Now I got it. "Is he going to have any more seizures?" I asked.

"Dr. Levy said since we're increasing the amount of medication that Mikey takes, he shouldn't have seizures anymore."

"OK, so no more seizures?" I asked again. I felt like Mikey since I was asking the same question over and over.

"Let's hope not, Katie," Mom said. "He has epilepsy. That means we can't predict what will happen. But we have great doctors helping us."

That made me feel better. I didn't want anything bad to happen to Mikey. "Mom?" I had one more question for her.

"Yes, Katie?"

"Is there any medicine the doctor can give Mikey so that he doesn't have autism anymore?" I held my breath and looked down at the floor as I waited for her to answer. I could hear my own heart beating.

She took a deep breath, as if her answer took a lot of courage to say. "There are no medicines that can take autism away, Katie," Mom answered.

"Oh, OK. I just thought it would be cool to know who Mikey would be without autism."

"I wonder about that, too, Katie," Mom said. "There are doctors and scientists all over the world who study autism. So who knows, maybe one day there will be some medications to help people with autism. We love Mikey for who he is and what he teaches us. And we support him by getting him the services he needs."

"What do you mean by 'services'? Do you mean speech therapy and physical therapy?" I asked.

"Yes, and social skills training, music therapy, and occupational therapy," she said. "There are other types of therapies, too and so many really great therapists and teachers out there who dedicate their lives to helping kids like Mikey."

That made me think about our old babysitter, Cate, who was studying to become a speech therapist.

"More, Erin! More! More!" Mom and I heard Mikey happily shout from the living room. We could hear Erin and Mikey laughing together. We both knew he was asking her to send him another email or text. We smiled at each other with a bit of relief in our eyes. Mikey was back to his regular self after the seizure scare from last night.

"Mom, Erin told me about the autism walk right here in Fairview City. It's on Labor Day weekend. Can we do it?" I asked.

"Yes!" Mom said. "I just saw a flyer for that walk at the neurologist's office this morning. I even took a picture of the flyer so I could tell you about it." She took out her phone and showed me the picture. "It sounds like the perfect event for our family."

"Can we get T-shirts for the walk?" I asked. "Erin's wearing her shirt from the walk last year."

"Sure. Does Erin know someone with autism?" Mom asked.

"Yes, her cousin, Emily," I told her.

"That must be why she's so good with Mikey," Mom said. "She really gets it."

From the living room, we heard Erin talking. "Mikey, I can write one more email, and then I have to go."

"Over and out?" Mikey asked her.

Those words, *over and out*, are the words Mikey uses to end his email exchanges with friends and family. Erin didn't know this yet. "What?" Erin asked.

"Over and out," Mikey told her. Three times of course.

Mom was about to go to the living room to explain it to Erin. But Mikey was able to get his point across. "You write 'over and out' on your last email."

"OK, Mikey. I will!" Erin told him.

Mom and I looked at each other with wide eyes. I knew we were both thinking the same thing. It was great that Mikey told Erin what he wanted in a regular sentence. Instead of having a meltdown. Instead of just repeating it three times.

Erin walked into the kitchen where Mom and I were sitting. "Well, I have to get going. My mom and I are going to hang up flyers in town today for the autism walk," Erin told Mom and me. "Did Katie tell you about the walk?"

"Yes, and I just saw one of your flyers in the waiting room at the doctor's office," Mom said. "How do we sign up?"

"We have a website where people can sign up and make donations." Erin told her how to find the site.

"Can we do anything to help with the walk?" Mom asked.

"Yes! Invite your friends and family. Your neighbors too. We like to get a lot of people involved," Erin explained.

"OK. We can get a crowd there for sure," Mom said. "Even though we're new here, we'll get our neighbors to sign up."

"Thanks for having me," Erin said as she opened the back door to walk home. "Katie, let me know when you want to make bracelets again!"

"I will," I replied.

"And let me know when you're done making those All About Autism cards," she continued.

"OK."

"I hope they're done soon so we can hand them out at the walk," Erin said. "Bye, Katie!"

"Bye, Erin!" Even though she was older than me, I felt like I made a good friend today. Someone who really gets it.

It was time to get to work on the cards. I had to get out my list book.

Ideas for the
All About Autism Cards
Page 1

People with autism:

- might act younger than their real age

- spin or flap when happy

- don't like crowded or noisy places

- are smart AND impulsive

- need a routine to feel safe

- have a hard time making eye contact

- no two people with autism are exactly alike

Page 2
(ideas for autism cards)

People with autism:

- have trouble understanding body language

- go to a lot of therapies like OT, PT, and Speech Therapy. They go because they have a different way of learning and the therapy sessions help them learn the best way for their brains and bodies

- have trouble with communication and answering questions

- communicate in a different way. Some people with autism are able to talk with words and some use a communication device to talk.

Chapter Seventeen
Creating the Cards

I asked Mom if I could invite Caroline over to help me work on the All About Autism cards. I knew Caroline would want to be involved, and I knew I needed her help.

"How do we get started on making the cards?" Caroline asked when we were in my room.

"Well, I've been thinking. First we have to decide what information to put on the cards," I said. "Facts about autism, I guess." I took out one of my list notebooks and a pen, prepared to start adding ideas to the lists I'd already started.

"Should we look it up online?" Caroline asked.

"Look what up online?" I asked.

"Facts about autism," Caroline said.

"That's a good idea," I said. But I had something

else in mind. "Before we look it up, I wanted to ask you something."

"Sure, ask me anything," Caroline replied.

"When you told me about going to your cousin's party the other day, you talked about your cousin's neighbor who has autism," I began.

"Yeah, his name is Matt," she reminded me.

"You said that you used to feel nervous to talk to Matt or play with him when you visited your cousin."

Caroline nodded.

"But then last time you went, you played with him. What was different this time?" I asked.

"Well, I think since you guys became our neighbors and I've been around Mikey, I get it that kids with autism are just like other kids. They like to play. They like to hang out. They might make different noises when they are happy or be interested in things that most kids aren't interested in," Caroline told me. "But they still like to swim and play and do anything other kids do."

As she talked, I wrote down some of what she was saying in my notebook. "Your ideas are good for the All About Autism cards," I told her.

"I used to be afraid to talk to kids who are different from me. I think that's because I didn't know any kids

162

with autism. Now I know Mikey, and I'm not afraid to talk to kids who are different from me," she said. "Actually, I really like talking to Mikey."

I was proud of Mikey. He was helping kids think more positively about autism. He was helping kids get it. Caroline said so herself.

"OK, we have a good start to our lists of what we can put on the cards," I told Caroline. I took out my iPad and typed in *autism facts* and then tapped *search*.

The iPad screen came up with a list of websites about autism facts. Just as I was about to tap on the first one, my iPad switched to the FaceTime screen telling me I had an incoming call from Lauren!

I tapped "accept call" and saw Lauren's and Bella's smiles on the screen. "Hi, guys!" I said. "Caroline, it's my friends from Connecticut! Come sit next to me so they can meet you."

Caroline moved closer to me so she could see the girls and they could see her. "Hey, Katie! Nice you meet you, Caroline," Lauren said.

Bella gave us her famous double thumbs-up and said, "Hello, New Yorkers!"

We all giggled at that.

Caroline smiled at them and waved hello as she quietly said, "Hi."

"What's up?" I asked.

"We're just checking in to see how the All About Autism cards are coming along," Lauren said. "You know we love to do projects together."

"It's so funny that you called now," I told them. "Caroline and I *just* started writing a list of ideas for the cards."

"Cool," Bella said. "What do you have so far?"

I read one of the lists from my notebook.

Page 3
(ideas for autism cards)

People with autism:

- are usually interested in one subject and like to talk about it

- have a hard time expressing their feelings

- like to hear certain words repeated or say the same things over and over

- like to see how things work like turning lights on and off, flushing toilets and pushing buttons

- may appear to have no awareness of danger - so safety rules should be reviewed a lot

"That's great," Bella said. "I think you should add something about invisible disabilities," she added.

"What does that mean?" asked Caroline.·

"Some disabilities you see right away, like me with

my walker," Bella explained. "And some you don't see right away. Those are called invisible disabilities."

Caroline nodded, but she still looked confused.

"You know," I said, "like how the ice cream man didn't believe that Mikey has autism because he can't see it. Good idea, Bella." I jotted it down in my notebook.

"Also, maybe something about how most kids with autism don't act their age," Lauren said.

That made me remember the first time I met Lauren's older brother, Jimmy. He's eighteen years old and has a disability. He was watching *Sesame Street* when I met him. I remember being surprised that he was watching a little-kid show. But now I get it.

"Should we add something about how some kids with autism are grabby?" asked Bella.

"What do you mean?" asked Lauren.

"I just know that Mikey likes to grab things," Bella said. "I remember playing the game Sorry with him in Lunch Bunch at school last year. He would always grab the game cards when it wasn't his turn. It doesn't mean he's trying to take something away or hurt anyone. He's just very impulsive."

"Good one, Bella," I told her as I added *impulsive and grabby* on the list. "Remember how Adam was so good at solving the Rubik's Cube?" I said.

"Who's Adam?" Caroline asked.

"He's a boy in our school who can solve the Rubik's Cube in two minutes or less. He has autism," Bella said.

"Yes, but not all people with autism can solve a Rubik's Cube," Lauren said. "So I don't think that should go on the list."

"But some people with autism do have a special skill that they can just do without being taught," I said. "Mikey has a classmate who memorizes calendars. If you tell him your birthday and year, he knows what day of the week you were born."

"Wow, that's cool!" Lauren said.

"Yeah, and my cousin's neighbor knows how to play any song on the piano after just hearing the song one time," Caroline said.

"Really? That's amazing!" Bella said.

"But not all kids with autism can do things like that," I reminded them. "Mikey has trouble wearing certain clothes. He won't wear jeans because they're not soft. And he won't eat ice cream because he doesn't like cold things in his mouth."

"Same with my cousin's neighbor!" Caroline said. "When I was there for a party, all the kids were eating ice pops, but he ate potato chips instead."

"I think we should add something about how kids with autism sometimes seem like they are in their own world," I said. "It looks like they are not listening to what's going on around them because they're focused on something else."

"Yes, like when Mikey watches the lifeguards change! He's definitely in his own world then," Caroline said.

"Let's add something about how kids with autism sometimes laugh at the wrong time, like when someone else is hurt or crying," Bella said.

"Good one, Bella," Lauren said. "And let's add something about how most people with autism don't like loud or busy places like the mall. But they do like to make loud noises sometimes."

"Yes, and how the noises they make might sound different than what we're used to hearing," Caroline said. "When I was playing with my cousin's neighbor in her pool, I didn't know if he was laughing or crying. Then he told his mom he was happy, so I knew it was laughter."

I could totally relate to that. Mikey makes loud sounds all the time, and it really is hard to tell if his noises are happy or sad—even for me, and I live with him.

"Most of all, we have to write something on the cards about how people with autism have feelings just like anyone else," Lauren said.

Caroline and I chatted with Lauren and Bella for a while longer. Caroline fit in so easily with my old friends. We told Lauren and Bella about the autism walk coming up at the end of the summer. "Oh, is that where you'll hand out the cards?" Bella asked.

"Yup, that's the plan," I told them.

"Wait, what's that on your wrist?" Bella asked me. "Hold your wrist in front of the camera so I can see your bracelet."

I held my wrist still in front of the camera.

"Where did you get those bracelets, Katie?" Bella asked. "They're so pretty."

"Thanks!" I couldn't believe they thought I bought the bracelets somewhere. "Actually, I made the bracelets this morning."

"Really?" Bella said. "Can you make one for me? Please?"

"Of course," I told Bella.

"You already know my favorite colors," Bella said. "Lauren, do you want one too?"

"Definitely," she said. "Do they take a long time to make?"

"Nope. Each bracelet only takes about ten minutes to make. I can teach you guys how to make them if you want?"

"Yes!" all three of my friends said at the same time. Then we all started laughing.

Lauren and Bella had to end the FaceTime call because they were getting ready to go back-to-school shopping. Now that it was just Caroline and me working on the All About Autism cards together in my room, she asked me about Mikey. "How's he doing today?" I didn't answer right away, so she went on, "You know, after the seizure yesterday."

"Much better," I told her. "He went to the doctor and they figured out the problem. He needs more medicine."

"I'm so glad he's OK," Caroline said. "When my brothers go to the doctor, it's usually just for a back-to-school checkup. I've never actually had to worry about my brothers' health."

"Mikey has a lot of doctors and goes to lots of appointments," I told her. "I guess that's part of the job having a brother with autism. I worry about things most kids don't."

We got back to work finishing up our list of facts for the All About Autism cards. The list was starting to get too long. We had to narrow it down and decide which information was most important to include on the cards. We were working hard until we were interrupted by the sound of the doorbell.

What I worry about as a
Little Big Sister

I worry about kids making fun of Mikey at his new school.

I worry about Mikey having another seizure.

I worry if he will be able to ever do things like ride a bike or drive a car.

I worry about him getting lost again.

I worry about him getting hurt if he runs into the street.

Chapter Eighteen
Bracelet Business

Mikey was screaming with excitement about the doorbell ringing. Mom had unlocked the door halfway so Mikey could open it himself. He did his triple hop when he saw it was Erin. She had a stack of light-blue paper in her hand. "Hi, Mikey!" Erin said.

"Why are you here?" Mikey asked. "No more doctor. No more doctor. No more doctor," he said with some fear in his voice.

"All done with the doctor for today, Mikey," Mom told him.

"Is Katie home?" Erin asked Mikey.

"Katie, Katie, Katie!" Mikey yelled. He didn't realize that Caroline and I were already halfway down the stairs.

"Hi, Erin." Caroline and I said at the same time.

"Hi, Katie." Erin looked behind me and saw Caroline. "Oh, hey, Caroline. Great to see you girls together."

"Why are you here?" Mikey asked again. Sometimes his questions sound so rude. But this is just the way his mind works. He says things without thinking about how it will sound to others.

"I have these papers for Katie," Erin said. She handed me the stack. "Katie, these are flyers for the walk. I usually hand them out to everyone on my street."

"OK, thanks," I said. "Should I start handing these out on my street soon?"

"Yes, you can even start today," Erin said. "I have to go. My mom is waiting for me to get home so we can go hang up the flyers in town."

We all said good-bye to Erin. Mom had to follow Mikey outside so he could watch Erin ride away on her bike. "Beep! Beep! Beep!" he called out to her, and Erin rang her bike bell for him.

Mom walked back inside and said, "Girls, I think you should give a flyer to Caroline's mom. I'm sure she would want to know about the autism walk."

"Yup, we were just about to do that," I told Mom.

"OK, good. You should also walk over to Pam's house and give a flyer to her. I think she and Meredith would want to go to the walk and bring Gavin."

"OK, Mom," I said as Caroline and I walked out the front door. I unlocked the door quickly and easily. Most things that are easy for me are much harder for Mikey, like unlocking a door and riding a bike. We walked through Caroline's back yard to get to her back door. Looking at her back yard reminded me of the first day in our new house—the day Mikey sat in their back yard while Mom was freaking out because she thought he was lost. I'm almost glad he did that now since it helped us meet Caroline's family right away and become fast friends.

Caroline and I walked into her kitchen from the back door. Her mom was chopping vegetables at the kitchen counter. "Hi, girls," she greeted us. "Do you want some carrots?" She pointed to the plate where she placed the vegetables as she chopped.

"Thanks, Mom, but we're busy," Caroline told her.

She turned around from the counter and looked at us. "Oh? What are you girls doing today?" She sounded truly interested.

I handed her the blue flyer about the autism walk. "Erin told me about an autism walk here in Fairview City. She organizes it with her mom," I told her.

Caroline's mom took a look at the flyer, "Oh yes,

I've heard of this," she said. "Is this what you're busy doing?"

"Erin asked us to give the flyers out on our street," I said.

"And I'm helping Katie make autism cards," Caroline said proudly.

"What are autism cards?" Julie asked.

"Small cards that have information about autism written on them. You know, to help people understand autism better," I explained.

"That's a great idea!" Julie said. "I wish I'd had something like that when I was a teacher. That would have helped the other students understand special needs better."

"That's what we're hoping our cards will do," I said. "We are calling them All About Autism cards."

"That is a great name for the cards." Julie smiled at me. She looked at the flyer again. "It says here that all the money raised from the autism walk will go toward Unified Theater, Unified Sports, and Best Buddies."

"Yes," I told her. "Erin told me the walk raises a lot of money for those activities."

"This is great! How do I sign up?" Julie asked.

I pointed to the website printed at the bottom of the flyer.

"OK, I'll sign up online right now," Julie said as

she turned to her laptop. "Are you doing anything else to raise money, Katie?" she asked.

"Like what?" I asked.

"Well, I've been admiring those bracelets you're wearing," she said. "Did you make those?"

"Yes, Erin taught me how," I told her.

"Well, what if you and Caroline made a bunch of those bracelets in autism awareness colors and sold them at the walk?" she suggested.

Caroline and I looked at each other and smiled. Sometimes moms actually have good ideas. We went back to my house to start working on the bracelets. Luckily, Erin had left her bag of strings for me to make more bracelets. I showed Caroline what to do. First choose four colors of string—this time, four shades of blue for autism awareness. Then, tie a knot at the top. Finally I showed her how to make the knots that would create the bracelet.

When Caroline was finished making her first bracelet, she looked at it and asked, "Do you think I should keep it or add it to the collection of bracelets that we're going to sell?"

"You should definitely keep it. It's your first bracelet," I said as I tied it on to her wrist.

"I was hoping you'd say that." She smiled as she admired her new bracelet.

We spent most of the afternoon making bracelets. When we ran out of blue string, we asked Mom to take us to the craft store to buy more.

"Katie, I wish I could take you right now. But I don't have anyone to watch Mikey, and he already had a rough day with his doctor appointment," she told me. "I don't think he can handle something else that's out of his routine today."

I knew Mom was right. Mikey does not do well with spur-of-the-moment ideas like going to the craft store. But I was still disappointed. Mikey and his autism always get in the way of what I want to do.

"Can we go to the craft store tonight when Dad is home?" I asked.

"Maybe," Mom said. But I could tell from her voice that we wouldn't be going to the craft store that night. "Have you given a flyer to Pam yet?" Mom asked.

Then I remembered that we still had work to do for the walk besides the bracelets. It was time to hand out the flyers on our street.

Things that are hard for Mikey
(but easy for me)

Opening locks on doors

Riding a 2-wheeler bike

Being safe (in the kitchen, crossing the street)

Waiting in a line

Looking at people's eyes when I am talking to them

Learning to talk

Asking appropriate questions

Chapter Nineteen
One Hundred Bracelets

Caroline and I walked toward Pam's house with the stack of blue flyers and the small bag of finished bracelets. It looked like Pam might have a friend visiting since there was a car parked in front of her house. We rang the doorbell anyway. Pam opened the door and greeted us.

"Hello, girls," she said in a quiet voice. "Gavin is having a session with his new speech therapist in the living room," she explained. "That's why I'm talking quietly."

I peeked inside the door and saw Gavin sitting with a woman who looked like she was playing with him. I've sat through enough of Mikey's speech therapy sessions to know that it looks like play, but actually she was teaching him how to talk.

"We wanted to give you this flyer," I said in a quiet voice as Caroline handed her the blue paper. "It's about the autism awareness walk on Labor Day weekend," I told Pam.

She read the flyer. "Oh, this looks like fun," she said. "I'll share it with Gavin's mom so we can go together. What does this mean?" she pointed to the bottom where it said all the money made at the walk would be given to the Unified Theater, Unified Sports, and Best Buddies programs in our town.

Caroline and I explained a little bit about Unified Sports, Unified Theater, and Best Buddies to Pam.

"I'm so glad Fairview City has these important programs," Pam said. "How do I sign up for the walk?"

I pointed to where the website address was listed. Then I took out the bag of bracelets and showed Pam. "We're also selling these bracelets," I told her. "The money we make will all go toward the walk."

"Did you girls make these bracelets?" Pam asked.

We both nodded.

"Wow, these are beautiful," Pam said. "I'll buy three. How much are they?"

"Um, one dollar?" I said hesitantly. Caroline and I hadn't discussed the price yet.

"Oh, I think you should charge more. You're raising money for a very important cause," Pam said.

"How much should we charge?" I asked.

"Well, how much money are you hoping to raise for the walk?" she asked.

Caroline and I hadn't discussed that yet either, but I knew we wanted to raise a lot of money. "Three hundred dollars," I said. Caroline looked at me and nodded in agreement.

"Do you think you can make a hundred bracelets before the walk?" Pam asked.

"We made ten bracelets this morning, and that only took about an hour," Caroline said.

"Do you think you can each make ten bracelets a day?"

We both nodded enthusiastically.

"Because if you each make ten per day, you'd have a hundred in five days." She smiled at us. She seemed just as excited about the bracelet project as we were. "If you sell one hundred bracelets and charge three dollars each, you'll meet your goal of raising three hundred dollars." She added, "When I was younger, I worked in a bank for many years. That's why I'm quick with numbers. I started taking care of Gavin after I retired from my job at the bank."

That explained her speedy math skills. "OK. Three bracelets at three dollars each. That will be nine dollars please," I told her. Caroline handed her three bracelets, and Pam handed us the money.

"Girls, maybe you can come back to play with Gavin later on this afternoon," she said as we turned to leave.

"OK," Caroline and I said at the same time as we walked out the door.

"Girls—can you wait a minute?" Pam asked as.
We nodded.

"OK, good. I have something for you," she said.

Caroline and I waited outside sitting on her front stoop. A minute later, Pam opened the door. She was holding a small bag. "Here, you might need this," she said as she handed the bag to me.

"What is it?" I asked.

"Take a look inside," she urged me with a warm smile on her face.

I opened the top of the bag and saw packages of string. It was the exact kind of string we needed to make bracelets!

"Thank you!" I said to Pam. "How did you know we needed this?"

"I didn't know," Pam said. "I guess it was a lucky coincidence." She went on, "I bought that string months ago to give my granddaughter while she was visiting me, but I forgot about it. So now it's for you."

We got lucky! It was just what we needed.

* * * * * *

That night after Mikey went to bed, when the house was quiet, I showed Mom and Dad the lists for the All About Autism cards. My friends and I came up with some long lists, so it took them a while to read the whole thing.

Mom held the list between her and Dad as they sat on the sofa so they could read it together. I watched them from a chair across from the sofa. Mom was smiling, and I saw her wipe her eyes.

"Mom, are you crying?" I asked.

"Happy tears," she told me. "I am just so proud of you for helping people understand better about autism."

"Katie, this is a great list!" Dad said. "Do you want me to bring it to work tomorrow to ask our graphic designer to put these ideas from your list onto a small card?"

I really wanted to figure out how to make the cards myself. But I knew Dad's graphic designer at work would be able to get the job done quickly. And we needed the cards done as soon as possible in time for the walk.

"Thanks, Dad. That's a great idea," I told him.

Things that are hard for ME

(but easy for Mikey)

Memorizing the garbage and
recycling schedule

Memorizing the school lunch menu

Taking medicine

Falling asleep early

Introducing myself to new people

Chapter Twenty
Lemonade

The next day, Caroline and I spent the entire morning at my house making bracelets with the string from Pam. We made bracelets till our fingers got tired. It was time for a break.

As I walked down the stairs to the kitchen for a snack, I could hear Mom talking on the phone. "Yes, the walk is over Labor Day weekend." She paused. I guess she was listening to whoever she was talking to. "Yes, it's right here in Fairview City, and you can sign up online. I'll text you the website." She looked up, saw me coming, and said in a hushed voice, "OK, I have to run, Katie's here. Talk to you soon!" She sure did rush off the phone.

"Who was that?" I asked as Caroline and I walked into the kitchen.

"Who was what?" Mom asked.

"On the phone."

"Oh, just one of my friends," Mom said. "I was telling her about the walk." Then she changed the subject. "Would you girls like a snack?"

"Yes," we both said.

Mom poured lemonade into two glasses and got out a bowl for popcorn.

I could hear Mikey in the living room talking very loudly on the phone to Nana. He loves talking to her every day. She's the only one who can get him to have a real conversation with actual details. She gets him out of his own world and sort of into our world when they have their daily phone conversations.

"Katie! I just got a really good idea!" Caroline said after taking a long sip of lemonade.

"Me too," I said.

"Let's have a lemonade stand!" we both said at the same time!

"Yes! And we can hand out flyers for the walk while we sell lemonade," Caroline said.

"All the money we make will go toward the walk," I said.

Mom opened the cabinet to get a large plastic pitcher for the lemonade. "I don't think we have any plastic cups for the lemonade stand," she said.

"I'll run home to get some. I know my mom has them." Caroline ran out the back door.

A moment later, Caroline was back with a stack of cups. We started setting up the table out front for our lemonade stand.

When Mikey got off the phone, he came out to see what we were doing. He started ringing neighbors' doorbells with Mom following close behind, telling them to come buy some lemonade. It worked! We had lots of customers.

It reminded me of selling Girl Scout cookies in first grade. I was so nervous to ring my neighbors' doorbells to ask them if they wanted cookies. Mom made me practice what I would say when neighbors opened their doors. It was something simple like, "Hi, I'm selling Girl Scout cookies. Would you like to buy some?" Mikey came with me to sell the cookies (Mom was there too, of course), and I remember when the neighbors would open their doors, he would say, "You are buying Girl Scout cookies from my sister." It was sort of rude, but sort of funny. And the best part was, I didn't have to say anything at all. It was the first time I remember feeling like my big brother was looking out for me.

When Mikey was done telling our new neighbors to come buy lemonade, he stayed outside as the Neighborhood Watch. The mail truck drove up our block, and the mailman started delivering mail. When he got to our house to deliver our mail, Mikey told him, "Buy lemonade, lemonade, lemonade."

The mailman ignored Mikey, but Mikey didn't give up. He handed the mailman one of our flyers. "What's this?" he asked.

Mikey looked at me. He didn't know what to say.

"It's a flyer about the autism walk here in Fairview City," I told him. "Maybe you can come."

He glanced at the flyer and said, "Nah, I work on Saturdays. I can't go to this thing." He started walking to the next house to deliver mail.

Mikey hopped behind him, saying, "Lemonade, lemonade, lemonade." He grabbed a cup and handed it to him.

"You don't have to pay for it," Mom told him. "It's such a hot day to work outside. Enjoy!"

"Thanks," he said as he took a sip. Mikey loves watching people eat and take sips of their drinks. He stood way too close to the mailman as he watched him drink his lemonade. Mikey was smiling with his whole body. He almost flapped the mailman's cup right out of his hands.

"Watch where you're going!" the mailman said in an angry voice to Mikey. "And don't touch my bag." He started walking away to deliver mail to the next house.

Mom opened her mouth to say something to the mailman but stopped. Instead, she turned to Mikey and said, "Good job, Mikey, handing out the flyer and the lemonade. That was a kind thing to do." She said it loud enough for the mailman to hear.

I wished our All About Autism cards were finished so I could give one to the mailman right now. I knew he really needed to read it.

By the end of the afternoon, we had sold six pitchers of lemonade and handed out all of the flyers. Our spontaneous idea was a success!

That night, after Mom put Mikey to bed and we had our quiet house, I told her all about the lemonade stand.

"Katie, I'm really proud of you," she told me. "We've only lived here for such a short time, and you're already making a difference in our neighborhood."

"Well, I've had a lot of help," I said. I was thinking of Pam giving us the string, and Caroline making the bracelets with me. I thought of Mikey getting us the lemonade customers and Erin giving us the flyers to hand out. "Mom, when the mailman was so rude to Mikey today, why didn't you say anything to him?"

"Good question, Katie." Mom said. "I was about to say something, but in the moment, I couldn't think of the right words to say to him. So instead, I decided to say something positive to Mikey."

Times When Mikey acted like a Big Brother

When he helped me sell Girl Scout cookies back when I was in 1st grade

Today when he helped us get lemonade customers by telling the neighbors to come buy some

I liked the way it felt, to have a big brother looking out for me

Chapter Twenty-One
Way to Go

The day before the walk, we woke up to weather that was so sunny and hot that Mom announced it was a pool day. She said I could invite Caroline to come with us.

When Mom drove into the pool's parking lot, it was already packed with cars. "Mom, can you drop Caroline and me off at the entrance while you and Mikey go park the car?" I asked.

"We won't have to walk far, Katie," Mom replied. "I'll use our blue sign to park close today."

Oh no. My excitement for arriving at the pool quickly shifted to an uncomfortable feeling in my stomach. Mom called Mikey's disability parking permit the "blue sign." She hangs it on her rear-view mirror when she parks in disability parking spots. I used to think that the blue signs were only for people who were in wheelchairs or people who couldn't walk far distances. But I found out that people with invisible disabilities, like Mikey, can also have disability parking permits.

I remember Mom told me that Mikey's doctor suggested she get the disability parking permit for his own safety. Mom needs it for Mikey because he runs away from her in parking lots, so parking close to entrances is safer for Mikey. Mom can use the permit at places like the pool, restaurants, or even doctor offices. Then Mikey doesn't have to cross any parking lot lanes to get to the entrance.

I know most people don't have the blue sign, and I was wondering if Caroline thought it was strange that we did. Mom found a disability parking space in the crowded parking lot right away, very close to the pool entrance. She hung the blue disability parking sign on her rear-view mirror.

I glanced at Caroline from the corner of my eyes as she watched Mom hang the blue sign. Mom explained, "We use this blue sign in parking lots so we can keep Mikey safe by parking close."

"Good idea," Caroline said. I can't believe I was nervous about what she would think. I should have realized that she would get it.

Walking in through the pool entrance was a lot easier now compared to our first day at the pool a few weeks ago. Going to the pool was becoming part of Mikey's routine. He knew what to expect, and when he knows what to expect, he usually doesn't have a meltdown.

As soon as we found pool chairs for our bags and towels, Caroline and I jumped right into the water. It felt great to cool off! We found Ella, and then the three of us went down the slides a few times. We hung out for a while and then went to get our towels for a break.

Mikey was sitting with Mom, watching the lifeguards change chairs as usual. As we got our towels, I heard Mikey tell Mom he wanted to go on the slides. "Slide time! Slide time! Slide time!"

Caroline heard him too. He was so loud I'm sure everyone around us did. Caroline said, "Mikey, do you want to go on the slides with us?"

The uncomfortable feeling arrived in the pit of my stomach again. I was glad Caroline offered but nervous that Mikey would be loud and embarrassing on the slides. I was also secretly wishing that today was David's day off.

"Yes! Yes! Yes!" Mikey said with a hop for each *yes*.

Mom gave me a look that asked *Is this OK with you?* I nodded *yes* back at her. She smiled. It's cool that Mom and I can communicate with just our eyes and facial expressions. Without words.

"OK, let's go, Mikey," Caroline said.

Mikey started half walking and half hopping over to the slides. Caroline, Ella, and I caught up to him and surrounded him. As we walked together, we reminded him of the rules.

"No running," Ella said.

"One person on the slide at a time," Caroline chimed in.

"Sit on your bottom and go feet first," I added. I think we all wanted to make sure Mikey knew the rules so that if David was working, he wouldn't get yelled at.

When we got to the stairs, I knew that taking Mikey on the slide with us was going to be a big mistake. It wasn't David's day off. Even from the bottom of the stairs, I could hear him yelling at the kids in line. "I said GO!" he yelled at a little girl in the front of the line. "Hurry up!"

The girl looked really scared. Maybe it was her first time going down the big slide. I felt bad for her. I wish I could've walked over to her to say something kind like *you got this* or *it will be fun*. But I knew if I walked over to her, David would yell at me for getting out of line.

As we got closer to the front of the line, I could see David looking at Mikey with an unfriendly look on his face. Mikey was so excited he was doing his triple hop and saying, "Slide time! Slide time! Slide time!"

"Stop jumping!" David yelled at Mikey.

Mikey didn't understand that David was yelling at him, so he kept jumping. He was in his own world where only his joy for the slide existed.

Again, David yelled, "I said, stop jumping. Can't you hear me?"

Caroline bravely stood up for Mikey. "Stop yelling at Katie's big brother."

David looked at us with his mean eyes. "Are you sure he's your *older* brother?" he asked. "He doesn't look—or act—older than you."

Ouch. That hurt my heart. I opened my mouth to say something, but no words came out.

"That's enough, David." It was Erin, coming up the steps, wearing the staff shirt. I thought she only worked in the snack bar, but I guess she works at the slide too.

"Oh, hi, Erin," David said with a smile. I had never seen him smile before. He totally changed the way his voice sounded, too. Erin was his age and very pretty. David was probably trying to pretend he was a nice guy. But I knew the truth.

"You shouldn't be yelling at these kids," she told him. "And insults are not part of the job."

"Um, what are you talking about?" he asked, trying to sound innocent.

"I can hear you yelling at these kids from the bottom of the stairs," she continued. "You sound like a big bully."

"I'm just telling them when it's their turn to go down the slide," he replied. "And making them follow the rules. I'm doing my job."

"No, you're saying things like 'hurry up' to little kids who are scared. And 'can't you hear me?' to kids who may have special needs." Erin paused. David was silent. "There's definitely a kinder way to talk to kids."

Erin took over as the attendant at the slide while David walked toward the stairs. But instead of walking down the stairs, David stood there and watched Erin as she worked. When it was almost Mikey's turn, she gave him a high five and said, "Have fun, Mikey!"

Next in line was a little boy all by himself. His wide eyes and worried forehead showed how scared he must have felt. Erin bent down and asked, "Is this your first time on the slide?" The boy nodded.

Erin said, "Just sit with your feet first, smile, and have fun!"

Immediately, I noticed the look of worry left the little boy's face as he took his turn to go down the giant twisty slide.

Caroline, Ella, and I went on the slide many more times that afternoon with Mikey. We always let him go ahead of us because he liked waiting for us at the bottom. He loved cheering us on as we came down the slide. He mixed up Ella's and Caroline's names, but they didn't mind. Only I cared about that.

The next time we were climbing up the slide steps, I noticed David was walking down. Mikey was saying, "Number six, number six, number six," since it was our sixth time going down the slide.

As David passed by, the girls and I looked away. We ignored him. But Mikey said, "What's your name, name, name?"

"I'm David," he said. "Are you Mikey?" His voice sounded kinder. Maybe he learned something from watching Erin.

"Yes! Yes! Yes!" Mikey loves meeting new people. Even people like David. Then he asked a real question. "Why are you going down, down, down? The slide is up, up, up!" Mikey took David's hand and led him back up the stairs. I guess in Mikey's mind, it just didn't make sense that someone would walk *down* the stairs instead of walking up to the fun slide.

David followed along. I don't know if he had a choice since Mikey was dragging him and wouldn't let go. When they got to the top of the stairs, Mikey asked his usual questions. I heard him ask how many more minutes till lifeguard change and what David planned to have for dinner that night.

"Probably pizza tonight," David replied. "OK, it's almost your turn, Mikey."

Erin was still the attendant on duty, and she said, "OK, Mikey. It's safe to go down now. Your turn!"

David high-fived Mikey and said, "Go, Mikey!"

Mikey turned and went down the slide. I could hear him repeating, "Go, Mikey! Go, Mikey! Go, Mikey!" to himself all the way down.

It reminded me of a moment at our old pool in Connecticut. They had a diving board there. Mikey would always walk out to the end of the diving board and take way too long before jumping in the pool. I think he was nervous. One day when the pool was really crowded, he was standing on the end of the board, taking too long to jump in. His favorite lifeguard, Cate, who was also our babysitter, started chanting his name, "MI-KEY! MI-KEY!" to encourage him to jump off. Soon the entire pool was chanting his name. He stood there on the diving board, clapping for himself as everyone chanted his name. Then, when he finally jumped in, the applause for him was incredible.

Erin smiled at David and said, "Go, David!" It almost sounded like she was cheering *him* on.

"What?" David asked. He must have thought she was telling him to go down the slide. "I'm not going down the slide. I'm not even wearing my bathing suit."

"I mean, '*Way to go!*'" Erin said.

"Way to go? About what?" David asked as I was stepping up to take my turn going down the slide. He had a confused look on his face.

"You changed your ways. You turned over a new leaf. I'm glad you learned how to treat Mikey with kindness," she explained.

I wanted to hug Erin or say thank you to her. I knew David learned it from watching the way she talked to Mikey and other kids. But it was my turn to go down the slide.

Erin said, "Your turn, Katie." I took my spot at the top of the giant slide. As I began sliding down, she said, "See you tomorrow at the walk!"

* * * * * *

Dad got home late from work that night. He was holding a box. "Special delivery for Katie," he announced.

He handed the box to me. It was about the size of a shoebox but felt much heavier than shoes. I wondered what was inside. As soon as I got the top open, I realized it was our All About Autism cards! Wow, that was fast—and the cards looked awesome!

"Dad! How did you get these done so fast?" I gave him a hug.

"Anything is possible in New York City." He winked at me. "Our graphic designer has a friend who owns a printing company. The owner of the printing company loved the cards so much she printed them quickly and for free!"

I couldn't wait to show Caroline, Lauren, and Bella how they turned out!

Thank you, Erin

She is making a difference in Mikey's world and in mine

She just knows how to spread kindness

She taught David a lesson about kindness that he needed to learn

Chapter Twenty-Two
Surprise Guests

The chime of our loud doorbell woke me up the next morning. I looked at the clock next to my bed and saw it was only 7:30 a.m. *Way* too early for someone to ring a doorbell. Especially on a Saturday.

Next, I heard Mikey shouting, "FedEx! FedEx! FedEx!" He loved delivery trucks of any kind.

Then I remembered what day it was. Autism Walk Day! I got dressed as quickly as possible. As I came downstairs for breakfast, Mikey came running over to me, holding something blue in his hand and yelling, "Katie, Katie, Katie!" He threw it up into the air at me and went back to the kitchen.

Luckily, the blue thing Mikey threw at me was soft, so I didn't get hurt when it landed on my feet. It was a T-shirt. I crouched down to pick it up, and as I held it up to look at it, I heard Dad say, "Ta-da!"

I looked up and noticed that Mom and Dad were both wearing the same blue shirt I was holding. Mom turned around to show me the back of the shirt. It said, "Team Mikey." The front said, "Shine a Light on Autism" and the year. Right away, I put my new shirt on over the tank top I was wearing.

"Wow! The shirts came out great! I totally forgot that we ordered them!" I said.

"I placed the order last week," Dad said. "And they arrived this morning, just in time for the walk."

So that's why the doorbell rang so early. The FedEx truck was delivering these awesome shirts!

Erin had asked Mom if we could arrive at the walk about an hour early to help set up. The plan was that Mom and I would drive over first. Then, Dad and Mikey would meet us there just before the walk started so Mikey wouldn't have to wait too long for the action to begin. We do that a lot. Go places in two cars, just in case Mikey has to arrive late or leave early.

When Mom and I were walking out the door to leave for the walk, Dad followed us out to the car and said, "Don't forget this," as he held the box of T-shirts.

"Oh, there are more shirts?" I asked. "For who?"

Dad had a strange look on his face that I couldn't figure out. He began to open his mouth to answer me, but Mom quickly replied for him. "The shirts are for anyone at the walk who wants to wear one. Neighbors and friends," she added.

Mom and I drove into the parking lot at the playground, and I noticed there were lots of cars there already. I recognized some kids from the Unified Theater production who were there helping out. Lifeguards from the pool were setting up tables along the edges of the playground for the food. Blue balloons were everywhere.

Erin greeted Mom and me with a hug. "Your shirts came out awesome!" she told us.

"Thanks, so did yours," I told her.

"Can you guys set up the bagels and coffee on this table?" Erin gestured to an empty table as we entered the playground.

"Sure!" Mom and I said together.

"Katie, when you're done setting up the breakfast table with your mom, you can be in charge of the balloons. Each table needs four balloons tied to it," Erin explained.

I nodded, glad to have a few jobs to keep me busy. Mom and I got the bagels arranged quickly, with tubs of butter and cream cheese next to them. Next, I started tying the balloons to tables. More and more people were arriving to set up and sign up for the walk.

Erin was walking around giving the other volunteers jobs to do. I overheard Mom talking to Erin's mom.

"She really enjoys planning this event," Erin's mom said. "Each year we bring autism awareness to more and more people."

"What a great way to help people understand more about autism. Did you see the All About Autism cards that Katie and her friends made?" Mom asked.

"Erin told me about the cards. What a great idea! I can't wait for the girls to hand them out today and use them in the community to help people get it," Erin's mom said.

"And I love how the money raised from the walk goes to the great programs right here in Fairview City," Mom added.

"That was Erin's idea when we first started the walk," Erin's mom said. "With the money raised from the walk last year, Unified Theater was able to buy new costumes for their shows. Unified Sports was able to buy new sports equipment, and Best Buddies used the money to have a dance with a DJ at the end of the school year!"

Just then, something pink caught my eye in the distance. It sort of looked like a small pink bicycle from far away. But as I looked more closely, I realized it was a pink walker. *Could it be? Was it possible?*

YES, it was Bella! I saw her huge smile coming my way! Lauren was right next to her. They saw me staring at them with my mouth half open in disbelief. I started running over to greet them.

I had a million questions for them as I hugged them both. "How did you get here? How did you find the walk? How long are you staying?" I saw their moms standing next to Bella's car waving at me.

"We're a team, Katie!" Lauren said.

"We'd never miss an important day like today!" Bella added.

Mom walked up behind us, holding a few blue T-shirts. She hugged the girls and their moms. "Welcome to New York!" she said as she handed out their shirts.

"Mom!" I looked at her. "Did you know they were coming?"

Her huge smile told me that she had made this happen.

The three moms stood together and talked as I led Bella and Lauren over to the playground area. I wanted to show them the table that I was just starting to set up with bracelets and the All About Autism cards. They both bought a bracelet and started reading the cards.

"These came out great, Katie!" Bella said. "I see my

idea here." She pointed to the part about invisible disabilities on the back of the card.

"You're going to help a lot of people get it about autism with these cards!" Lauren said.

"We," I said. "*We* are going to help a lot of people. I couldn't have done any of this without you guys. And Caroline too!" I couldn't wait for Caroline to arrive so I could introduce her to Lauren and Bella.

Today's Surprises
(so far)

Bella and Lauren came all the way from Connecticut for the Autism Walk!

Our Team Mikey shirts came out awesome (I forgot all about them)

Chapter Twenty-Three
And the Winner Is...

"Where's Mikey?" Bella asked. "I don't see him anywhere."

"He'll be here soon," I told her. "Dad's going to bring him just before the walk begins. Then he doesn't have to wait too long for things to get started. Mom and I came early to help set up."

"Oh yeah, I remember how much Mikey hates to wait." Bella nodded at me.

I looked up and saw Caroline and her mom walking toward our bracelet table. She was holding the sign we'd made about buying bracelets. We were going to hang it on the table.

Mom had put our T-shirt box under the table, and I pulled out shirts for Caroline and Julie. "Put these on and join the team!" I greeted them.

"Good morning, Katie," Julie said as she gave me a hug. She and Caroline put their shirts on over their tank tops.

I introduced my old friends to my new neighbors. "It sort of feels like we already know you," Bella told Caroline.

"Yeah, since we've talked on FaceTime," added Lauren.

Caroline smiled and agreed with my old friends.

"Good morning everyone," I heard Erin's voice coming out of a speaker. I looked over and saw her holding a microphone. "Thank you all for being here to help set up for our fifth annual Shine a Light on Autism Awareness Walk!"

The volunteers and families all started clapping and cheering.

Erin went on to explain the schedule for the morning and that the walk would be starting in about twenty minutes. "If you haven't had a chance to get a bagel or coffee yet, please come on over to the breakfast table," Erin continued. "There are also awareness bracelets and car magnets to buy this year. Remember, all the proceeds go to our local programs."

More clapping.

"Thank you for your support! I'll start calling the teams to line up soon," Erin concluded.

"Erin! Erin! Erin!" I could hear Mikey's voice. He and Dad must have arrived just in time to hear Erin's announcement. They were already in their blue shirts. He ran over to Erin and gave her one of his extra-long Mikey hugs. When he tried to grab the microphone, I felt my stomach flutter, but Erin must have known he would do that. She passed the microphone quickly to her mom, who turned it off and put it away.

"Mikey, I have someone very special that I want to introduce you to," Erin said. "This is my cousin, Emily."

"Emily! Emily! Emily!" Mikey said. "Now I know three Emilys!"

Emily pushed a button on her talker that said, "Nice to meet you."

I thought Mikey was going to touch the buttons on Emily's talker, but he surprised me by giving her a quick high five and then asked her his usual questions. Once he found out what time she woke up and what she had for dinner last night, he turned to walk over to our table. When he saw Bella and Lauren, his mouth dropped open. "Why are you here?" he asked. I *wish* he had said, "I'm so glad you're here," or something more appropriate. But I also know that Lauren and Bella totally understood that he didn't mean to sound rude. They know he just says what's in his head without thinking about how it will sound to others once the words are out of his mouth.

"We're here for the walk!" Lauren told him.

"We even have shirts with your name on the back," Bella added. She and Lauren turned around to show him their backs.

"Team Mikey! Team Mikey! Team Mikey!" he repeated as he read their shirts.

He finally gave them each a hug. When he saw Julie, he immediately asked, "What's your phone on?"

"One hundred percent!" She smiled at him.

That news made Mikey do his triple hop and flap at the same time. He was smiling with his whole body.

"I wanted to make sure I had a full battery so I could take pictures and videos of all the fun today," Julie said.

Mikey started to wander away, and Dad followed him. "I'm on Mikey duty," he called out to Mom. She gave him the OK sign with her fingers

"Wow, you guys already sold a lot of bracelets." Mom had walked over to our table with Lauren and Bella's moms. She introduced Julie to them.

"We only have fifteen bracelets left," Caroline told her.

"I think you'll sell out for sure," Julie said.

"I'd like to buy three," Bella's mom said.

"Me too," added Lauren's mom. "We didn't drive all this way to go home without some of your famous bracelets!"

Caroline handed them the bracelets and put their money in the zippered pouch we'd been using as a cash register.

"What's that?" I asked Mom as I pointed to a blue thing she was holding in her hand.

"It's a car magnet," Mom said. She held it up, and I saw it was in the shape of a puzzle piece. In the middle of the puzzle piece, the words "Different—Not Less" were printed. Along the bottom were the words "Autism Awareness."

Erin's idea came out great! I really liked it and couldn't wait to put it on our car. I noticed Lauren's and Bella's moms were also holding the car magnets.

Erin was back on the microphone announcing that it was time to start the walk. I looked around. The playground was packed with a huge crowd of people. "It's time to start lining up. Please get together with your team and listen for your team's name to be called," Erin explained. "Team Emily will lead the way!" There was lots of clapping and cheering from the crowd.

Erin's family and friends gathered in their Team Emily shirts. They had a team of about twenty-five people, and they all stood in front of the giant banner that said "Shine a Light on Autism." A professional photographer from the local newspaper was there to take pictures of each team next to the banner.

Erin started calling out all the teams alphabetically. I saw Pam and Meredith were there with Gavin in his stroller. I recognized lots of people from our block. Mom and Dad were quickly handing out the Team Mikey shirts to our neighbors and friends. It was cool to see so many people there for Mikey.

I felt something brush up against my leg. It was Lucky, giving me a doggie kiss! "Hi, Ella! I'm so glad you guys are here," I said as I kneeled down to pet Lucky behind his ears. Ella was there with her mom and little brother. Dad gave them their shirts and he even had a really small one for Lucky to wear.

When I heard Erin announce that it was time for Team Mikey to line up, I was so excited. Dad helped Mikey lead everyone to the banner for our team picture. We had a huge group all wearing Team Mikey shirts. Mikey stood in the middle of our team and did his double thumbs-up pose for the picture.

The walk was a loop that started at the playground, went through a neighborhood that led to the main street of Fairview City, and then went back to the playground. Along the walk, there were people cheering us on. My friends and I had our pockets full of All About Autism cards to hand out to the people watching the walk.

I could hear Mikey reading the backs of all the shirts that he could see in front of us. "Team Emily," he said three times. "Team Joshua." "Team Peter." "Team Nicole." He read each three times, in his very loud and excited voice. I didn't feel embarrassed, though. We were with people who got it about Mikey and autism. Or who wanted to get it.

As we were nearing the end of the walk and almost back to the playground, I saw a mailman walking door to door, delivering mail. He stopped to watch what was going on, and I realized he was *our* mailman. I moved to the left side of the street where he was watching from the sidewalk. I wanted to be sure he got one of our cards today since he was one of the main people I had in mind when creating the cards.

I handed out a few autism cards to people standing near the mailman and then put one in his hand. He looked at it quickly and put it in his pocket. I hoped he would read the whole thing later.

The rest of the morning was awesome, I totally understand why Erin said this is her favorite event. We sold all of our bracelets! We ate, watched the magician, and just hung out.

Erin was holding the microphone again. "I just wanted to thank everyone again for coming today! I'd also like to recognize the team that raised the most money for the walk." She looked at her notes. Then she looked at me with a warm smile. "Let's give a round of applause to our fundraising leader, Team Mikey!"

I couldn't believe my ears. Did Erin really just say that Team Mikey raised the most money for the walk?

I looked around, everyone was cheering. Caroline and Lauren were jumping up and down. So was Bella while holding on to her walker. Of course, Mikey was jumping from hearing his name on the microphone! I joined them in the jumping and cheering. Mom and Dad came up behind me and gave me a hug.

Erin continued, "Members of Team Mikey did something more than just raising a lot of money for our local programs."

I could feel my face getting red. I didn't know what she was going to say next. *Why do I get embarrassed so easily?*

"Members of Team Mikey also did the most to raise autism awareness in our community," Erin said as she held up one of our All About Autism cards. "Katie, Caroline, Bella and Lauren—will you girls please come over here to stand by me?"

The four of us walked over to where Erin was standing. I felt my stomach do flips, and I hoped she wouldn't ask me to speak into the microphone.

"I'd like to say a giant thank you to these four girls who worked together to create the All About Autism cards." The crowd clapped. "If you didn't get one of the cards yet, please be sure to visit one of the girls before you leave," Erin told the crowd as she held up one of our cards again. "Next time you have to explain autism to a stranger, this card is a great tool to use."

The whole crowd gave us a huge round of applause with whistles and cheers.

"Go, Katie! Go, Katie! Go, Katie!" I heard Mikey say into the microphone. He had walked over to stand next to Erin, but it was really because he loves microphones. Everyone laughed, but instead of feeling embarrassed like usual, I laughed too. Mikey could be sort of funny sometimes!

All About AUTISM

Aware: It's hard for me to be **aware** of what my body is doing, so I may bump into you by accident or get too close when talking to you.

Unexpected: I may behave in **unexpected** ways. I might spin my body or flap my hands when I'm excited. Sometimes I make loud, unique sounds to express my feelings.

Talk: Please **talk** to me like you'd talk to any other friend my age. The way I **talk** may sound different from what you're used to. I might not look at you when you are talking to me, but I am aware of what you're saying. I may repeat words I've memorized from a show.

Inclusion: Get involved with me in activities that **include** everyone such as Best Buddies, Unified Sports, Special Olympics and Unified Theater.

Senses: My five **senses** are the same as yours, but I experience the senses differently. Sometimes I need a sensory break so I wear headphones, turn off bright lights or leave crowded places.

Make my day: Say hello to me and use my name.

Chapter 24
Beep Beep Beep

Three days had passed since the walk, and I was still smiling from it. I was already looking forward to next year's walk.

School would start tomorrow, so today was the last official day of summer vacation. I wanted to spend the day at the pool with my new friends as an end-of-summer celebration. Mom said she would take us, so I was getting my pool bag ready after breakfast.

The doorbell rang as I was putting my towel into my pool bag. Mikey got there first to open the door. Mom and I were right behind him. Mom helped Mikey unlock the door so he could turn the knob to open it himself. Our mailman was there holding a package in his hands. Mom, Mikey, and I all took a step outside.

"Special delivery for your sister," the mailman said as he handed it to Mikey.

"Katie, Katie, Katie!" Mikey hollered.

"Yes, will you please give it to her?" he asked.

Mikey turned and handed the box to me.

The mailman reached into his pocket and pulled out our All About Autism card. He looked at Mom and me and said, "I learned a lot from this card. I heard you are responsible for these?"

I couldn't believe my ears. I was speechless, so I just nodded my head.

"Yes, my daughter and her friends created them," Mom replied.

"Well, I was wondering if you have any extras?" he asked. "I want to give these to my friends who work at the post office. And some to other letter carriers."

The box of extra cards was on the table right inside the front door. I went in to get the box and came right back outside. "How many would you like? I asked.

"About twenty-five," he replied.

As I started counting out the cards, Mom asked him, "I heard you say *letter carrier*. Is that what I should be saying instead of *mailman*?

"Yes. My job through the post office is a letter carrier. Most people say mailman, though. They just don't realize the proper name."

"Well, I just learned something new from you too," Mom said. "Thank you."

I handed him the cards, and he put them into his pocket. "Thanks." He paused and then asked, "Did everyone who lives in the neighborhood get one?"

"Only the neighbors who came to the walk got one," I replied.

"Well, I can deliver one to each house in the neighborhood while I'm on my route today," he offered.

"That would be great!" I said. Mom nodded in agreement.

"Do you know anyone who would be a good helper?" he asked as he looked at Mikey and then smiled and looked at Mom. "Do you think Mikey would want to help me deliver the cards in your neighborhood?"

Mikey started jumping and flapping. That's how I knew he understood what was just said. "Yes, Mommy!" he said. "Mikey the Mailman! Mikey the Mailman! Mikey the Mailman!"

"Mikey the letter carrier," Mom smiled.

Mikey got his shoes on, and Mom followed behind as they walked with the letter carrier to deliver the All About Autism cards to most of the houses on our street.

I went inside with my package. I couldn't wait to

see what it was. Once I opened the box, I knew it would be something special because the card was from Lauren and Bella. The gift was a framed picture from the walk. A picture of Lauren, Bella, Caroline, and me together. All of us in our blue autism walk T-shirts. *Wow, they mailed that to me so quickly.* I ran up to my room to find just the right spot for it.

When Mom and Mikey came back from delivering the cards with the letter carrier, they were sweaty from being out in the summer sun. "Time to go to the pool," Mom said. "Katie, do you want to see if Caroline or Ella can meet us there?"

"I already asked them, and they both can," I told her.

When we got to the pool, we walked past the staff office. I saw Joe, the lifeguard we had met on our first day at the pool. He was waving at us.

"Joe! Joe! Joe!" Mikey said as he saw him walking over to us. "How many more minutes till lifeguard change?"

"About twelve minutes, Mike, and I'm going up to chair number three." I liked how Joe already knew what Mikey's next question would be and that he always calls him Mike. "Do you want to walk me to my chair when it's time?"

"Yes! Yes! Yes!" Mikey screamed.

As we walked over to our usual pool chairs, I heard Joe say to Mom, "I read in the local newspaper about the autism walk and the All About Autism cards. Congratulations!"

"Thanks, Joe," Mom replied. "Katie and her friends did a lot of work to create the cards."

"I was wondering if you have any extra cards?" Joe asked. "I think some of the people on my staff could learn a lot from those cards."

Wow, it was the second time in the same day that someone was asking for more cards. I couldn't believe it!

"Sure," Mom told him.

"OK, great!" Joe said. "I think I told you I'm a special education teacher during the school year. I might bring some to my school if that's OK with you."

"Of course!" Mom and I said together.

"Joe, it's time, time, time," Mikey told him.

"Yup, you're right, Mike," Joe replied as he looked at his watch. "Are you ready to walk me over to lifeguard chair number three?"

Mikey happily hopped over to Joe, took his hand, and walked him to the lifeguard chair.

My friends and I decided to go down the giant

slides since the line wasn't long yet. "Let's wait for Mikey to get back from walking Joe over to his chair," Caroline said. "He loves the slides too!"

Mikey was half walking and half hopping back to where we were waiting for him. That's the way he walks when he is super excited and trying not to run. My stomach did a flip when I saw that David was about to walk past Mikey. I was ready to hear him yell at Mikey to stop hopping. But he surprised me by high-fiving Mikey as he passed by. Wow, I guess he really learned the right way to treat others from Erin.

We had a great last day of summer at the pool and stayed as late as Mom would let us. When it was time to go home for dinner and get ready for school the next day, I was exhausted.

After dinner with my family, I heard the ice cream truck's music. I was tired, but never too tired for ice cream! The truck parked right in front of our house, and kids from our neighborhood were already starting to line up. Everyone was trying to hold on to one last night of summer. Once school started and we had homework and after-school activities, I don't think the ice cream truck would come around much anymore. Dad and I walked outside together for ice cream with Mikey and Mom following behind us.

"Same puzzle! Same puzzle! Same puzzle!" Mikey was shouting. None of us knew what he was talking about until he ran over to the ice cream truck and touched the car magnet. I couldn't believe my eyes! The ice cream truck had one of the "different—not less" puzzle piece magnets from the walk on his truck! Mikey is really good at noticing new things. Mom sometimes calls him "eagle eyes" because he is the first to notice when someone gets new glasses or a haircut. But today his eagle eyes noticed the puzzle piece magnet.

"Cool, Mikey!" Dad said. "The ice cream truck has the same puzzle magnet that Mom and I have on our cars. It's from the walk. Remember?"

"What's from the walk?" I heard someone behind me ask while I stood on the line to buy my ice cream.

It was Erin! She was pushing Gavin in his stroller. "Hi, Katie! I'm babysitting for Gavin while his mom and grandma are at a meeting with his new teacher. He's starting preschool tomorrow!"

My whole family greeted Erin and Gavin. Dad treated them to some ice cream. Mikey ordered for us all and when he said, "Thank you," the ice cream man replied right away with, "You're welcome, buddy!"

The smile on Mikey's face was one of the brightest smiles I have ever seen.

When I looked up at the ice cream man, I saw he had our All About Autism card taped to the window where customers place their orders.

Dad asked, "Where did you get this?" and pointed to the card. I think Dad and I were both shocked that he had it.

"There's a letter carrier I know who buys ice cream from me. I usually see him in this neighborhood. He gave the card to me this morning," the ice cream man replied.

"My daughter and her friends made those cards," Dad told him as he put his arm around my shoulder. "I know she wanted to give one to you, but I'm so glad you already have one."

"Oh, these are from you?" He looked at me as he pointed to the card. "Good job. Do you have any more of these? I want to give some to my friends who drive ice cream trucks and other food trucks."

I could not believe what was happening. The people who really didn't get it about Mikey were asking for more All About Autism cards.

"Sure, I'll go get some," I told him. I ran inside and grabbed a stack to give him.

"Thanks," he said as I handed him the cards. "I really used to think your brother was just being rude.

Thanks for teaching me. I don't like reading books, so this card is perfect for me."

Mikey was standing nearby. "Katie, say it, say it, say it!"

"Say what, Mikey?" I asked

"You're welcome!" Mikey told me.

Mom, Dad, and I smiled. Then I said, "You're welcome, you're welcome, you're welcome," to the ice cream man as he drove away, beeping his horn.

Mikey was smiling with his whole body.

Making a Difference

The All About Autism Cards
are working! More and
more people are getting it
about autism just from
reading the card we made!

People asked us for extra
cards - I can't believe it!

I think we might have to
order more cards soon

Finally! The ice cream man
gets it! So does the letter
carrier - and even David!

227

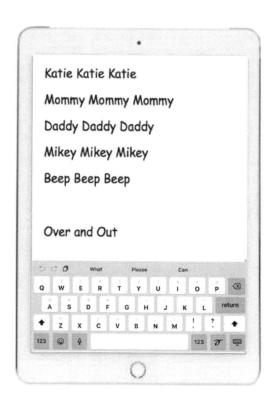

Katie Katie Katie

Mommy Mommy Mommy

Daddy Daddy Daddy

Mikey Mikey Mikey

Beep Beep Beep

Over and Out

(Mikey's List!)

QUESTIONS FOR THE AUTHOR, AMY MCCOY

WHERE DO YOU GET IDEAS FOR YOUR BOOKS?

Since my books are realistic fiction, I get my ideas from the world around me. Most of my ideas come from observing my own children's lives and from remembering moments from when I was a teacher.

WHAT INSPIRED YOU TO WRITE THE *LITTLE BIG SISTER* BOOK SERIES?

When my daughter was in second grade, I realized it was becoming difficult for her to have new friends over for playdates because her older brother with autism didn't act like a big brother. He made unexpected noises, needed extra attention, and didn't act like most big brothers. I decided to write a book so her friends could read it and understand what life is like for a sibling who has a brother or sister with autism.

WHERE DO YOU WRITE YOUR BOOKS?

I write anywhere it's quiet. I've written at the library, my dining room table, and sometimes on airplanes!

WHAT DO YOU ENJOY MOST ABOUT BEING A CHILDREN'S AUTHOR?

I enjoy being creative and making ideas come to life in books. I also enjoy going to elementary schools as a visiting author and spending time with students who like learning about the writing process.

HAVE YOU ALWAYS BEEN AN AUTHOR, OR HAVE YOU HAD ANY OTHER JOBS?

After I graduated from college, I was a teacher for many years. I taught almost all of the elementary grades. While I was teaching, I went to graduate school to became a reading teacher. I wanted to help kids who had trouble learning to read. I still keep in touch with some of my former students!

WHY DO YOU INCLUDE KATIE'S LISTS AT THE END OF EACH CHAPTER?

I am a list person myself. I've been making lists every day since I was a kid. I wanted to show Katie's lists at the end of each chapter to help readers get to know her inner thoughts.

Acknowledgments

To all the students who have read *Little Big Sister* and asked, "When are you writing a second book?" Thank you for your gift of motivation.

To the elementary schools, bookstores, Girl Scout troops, and community groups who have hosted me as a visiting author: thank you for giving me a platform to raise disability awareness.

To our neighbors, babysitters, camp counselors, teachers, and friends in Connecticut and New York: thank you for always beeping your horns for Matthew and for keeping him busy playing "the texting game".

Friends and professionals who offered content ideas for the All About Autism cards: Kerry Branca, Danielle Cameron, Theresa DeMarco, Crissy Dickey, Tania Egan, Lauren Kearney, Kara Leandro, Makenzie Sandler, Stephanie Smith, Meg Strickland and Theresa Zilins.

Kelly Cozy, my skilled and efficient copy editor, who found and fixed everything I overlooked.

To all of the teachers, speech therapists, paraprofessionals, teacher aides, coaches, nurses, doctors, OT's, PT's, school psychologists, teacher assistants, cafeteria workers, bus drivers, bus attendants, music therapists and school administrators who have positively influenced my children's lives– it takes a village. Thank you for being a part of our village.

My business coach, Stephanie Tishler, who inspires me to work hard and continue becoming who I'm meant to be.

My beta readers and dear friends for their thoughtful feedback of an early draft of this book: Trish Butler, Debbie DeBettencourt, Peggy Earnest, Meredith Fochetta, and Andrea Rhodes. Your friendship and feedback fill my heart and keep me moving forward.

Christine Maichin, wonderful friend and brilliant artist, who created the illustrations with tons of enthusiasm for this book.

My sister, Debbie DeBettencourt—for the long, late-night phone calls when we edited this book page by page. For your unending support and love—I hit the sibling jackpot!

To my parents, Sue and George Bashian—for instilling in me a love of reading and writing and for their everlasting support and love.

My children, Matthew and Kathryn, for inspiring me each day with their strength, confidence, humor, and love, and for giving me chapter ideas simply by living their lives and allowing me to create realistic fiction based on their reality.

My husband, Greg, for encouraging me to continue writing and for understanding the late nights of writing and editing. I wouldn't be able to do any of this work without your love and support.

—ABM

Unified Theater

Unified Theater dissolves typical barriers between youth through transformative, school-based performing arts programming. In Unified Theater, young people with and without disabilities, of all backgrounds, come together as equals to put on a production. The production is entirely organized, written, and directed by the students themselves. The concept is simple: empower youth to lead, let creativity rule, and put the Spotlight on Ability.

For more information, please visit kit.org

Special Olympics and Unified Sports

Special Olympics is dedicated to promoting social inclusion through shared sports training and competition experiences. Unified Sports joins people with and without intellectual disabilities on the same team. It was inspired by a simple principle: training together and playing together is a quick path to friendship and understanding.

In Unified Sports, teams are made up of people of similar age and ability. That makes practices more fun and games more challenging and exciting for all. Playing sports together is one more way that preconceptions and false ideas are swept away.

Visit playunified.org and specialolympics.org

Best Buddies

Best Buddies is the world's largest organization dedicated to ending the social, physical and economic isolation of the 200 million people with intellectual and developmental disabilities (IDD). Best Buddies programs empower the special abilities of people with IDD by helping them form meaningful friendships with their peers, secure successful jobs, live independently, improve public speaking, self-advocacy and communication skills, and feel valued by society.

To find a program in your area, please visit bestbuddies.org

Spread the Word

Founded by two youth leaders in 2009 as "Spread the Word to End the Word," the campaign focused its first 10 years on addressing a particularly powerful form of exclusion: the word "retarded". Over 10 years, leaders and self-advocates collected millions of digital and physical pledges to end the R-word. Each of these pledges was a personal commitment to acknowledge the hurt caused by the R-word and to be respectful in the words and actions taken towards people with intellectual and developmental disabilities.

In 2019, "Spread the Word to End the Word" became "Spread the Word," with a focus not just on the elimination of a word but on the creation of a new reality: inclusion for all people with intellectual and developmental disabilities. The campaign remains committed to empowering grassroots leaders to change their communities, schools, and workplaces, now through a call to their peers to commit to taking action for inclusion. With this change, Spread the Word will give community leaders for inclusion around the world the tools the needed to create change in their local circumstances.

For more information, please visit spreadtheword.global

About the Author

Amy B. McCoy is a former elementary school teacher who began writing for children in the 1990s. She is a visiting author to elementary schools and a disability educator working with both student and parent groups. Her mission with the *Little Big Sister* book series is to help students who are growing up with a sibling who has a disability to know they are not alone. She enjoys teaching yoga, spending time with her family and friends, traveling, and reading. Amy lives with her family in New York.

littlebigsisterbook.com

About the Illustrator

Christine Thompson Maichin has been drawing and painting since her dad put a paintbrush in her hand when she was five years old. Her professional experiences as Art Director for Nytimes.com and Design Director at Time Inc. led her to co-author and illustrate several books in the genres of fiction, non-fiction and graphic design. She enjoys spending time with family and friends, cooking delicious meals, taking long walks with her Wheaton spaniel, and sunsets at the beach. She lives in New York with her family.